NIGHT OF THE SNAKE

Snehaprava Das

BLACK EAGLE BOOKS
Dublin, USA | Bhubaneswar, India

Black Eagle Books
USA address:
7464 Wisdom Lane
Dublin, OH 43016

India address:
E/312, Trident Galaxy, Kalinga Nagar,
Bhubaneswar-751003, Odisha, India

E-mail: info@blackeaglebooks.org
Website: www.blackeaglebooks.org

First International Edition Published by
Black Eagle Books, 2023

NIGHT OF THE SNAKE
by **Snehaprava Das**

Cover & Interior Design: Ezy's Publication

ISBN- 978-1-64560-385-6 (Paperback)
Library of Congress Control Number: 2023936831

Printed in the United States of America

Snehaprava Das's amazing control over the bizarrely dramatic, meshed inextricably with her deep compassion for the desperately deprived, coming through a story like Night of the Snake presents a serious writer with a distinct voice. Her dexterity in handling disparate themes and appropriate techniques becomes evident in the story A Fairy Tale, seemingly an allegory. Elemental fury, manifest in a cyclonic storm that took away a child's parents , rendering her an orphan keeps coming back to haunt her in the orphanage and later in her adoptive home, in A House for the Doll, bringing the reader into the heart of human predicament in a disaster-prone region. Blue Umbrella tells the sombre tale of the tell-tale effects of the recent departure of the mother on her son, who tries to preserve her memory through a keepsake. The stories in this in this collection uphold her as a story writer of a high order in the English language.

A.J. Thomas
Former Editor , Indian Literature
Sahitya Akademi

The stories in this collection are atmospheric yet lucid, specific yet timeless, and they are built around the sad and tender idea that we as human beings are at best granted brief moments of beauty and peace. The language is deceptively simple and has a way of sneaking up on the reader quietly.

Nirmal Kanti Bhattacharjee
Writer, Translator and Editor of Niyogi Books

Night of the Snake is a collection of fifteen gripping and poignant tales about the complexities of human existence. The subjects chosen are multifarious in nature rangingfrom social to spiritual, and psychological to supernatural. They are intense and lyrically evocative and have the power to keep the reader seriously and aesthetically engaged.

Bhaskar Parichha
Writer, Editor, Critic and Journalist

DEDICATION

In the Hands of my Beloved Parents

CONTENTS

From the author's pen....

To the question why must a story be read, the obvious answer seems to be that a story is read primarily because it entertains us. It also keeps us engaged both emotionally and intellectually and impacts our thinking in manifold ways. So, that explains, partially though, the need of story writing, to keep the readers emotionally engaged, to entertain them. But a novel or a play too entertain and emotionally influence and, a poem, exercises an emotional hold over the readers. How, then is the experience of story reading different? It is indeed an intriguing question. You can say a poem is cryptic and compressed in nature and leaves most of things to the reader's imagination and ability of interpretation, while a novel is more or less, elaborative and descriptive in nature. A story could be in a way, a blend of the elements of all these. It could be an uncomplicated, unpretentious narrativizing of facts and at the same time could be arcane, intricate, leading the readers to a 'figure it out for yourself' point, and most importantly, it has an immediacy of effect. It does not keep the readers waiting, expecting, and speculating.

A story could usher us in to a world inhabited by real people, people of flesh and blood who breathe, laugh and cry, are genuine and fake, good and evil. We often meet there characters, living a life fraught with an amalgamation of shambolic emotions with whom we can connect, even identify ourselves.

'I am writing my story so that others might see fragments of themselves...' says Lena Waithe. Stories build up a world where the stakes and conflicts grip us and the emotions move us.

Here we are introduced to the socio-cultural milieu, sometimes familiar and strange at others, pleasant or somber, of lighter vein and serious, sometimes growing more nuanced with a fine juxtaposition of reality and fantasy, of the description of the visible contours of life and the exploration of the psychological depth of the characters.

Story tellers pick up a wide variety of characters from different professions and social classes prompting the readers to discover a relatability through a realization that in life things never turn out exactly as one thinks they will, to accept the reality of the disillusioned existence. They depict human emotions like love and sacrifice, hope and deceit and write about the human predicament designed by an inscrutable fate that brings upon a sudden, unexpected turn of events. They are efforts to locate man's plight in a world of uncertainties, his struggle to survive the odds with the force of an indomitable will. Stories too, reflect the writer's ideological position through themes of religion, loneliness, death and decadence. Stories could be about defining the visible world and people in it and the problems they are ridden with, or they could be like what Kafka believes an exploring into the inner conscious beneath a chaotic mess of outer realities. They could be morbid yet compelling tales of thoughts and incidents that do not make any sense on the surface but convey a whole lot of meaning and can lift the mind into a sublime state. Because of their exclusivity that does not allow entry the physical reality into the zone of elucidation, such stories do not follow a conventional pattern but are structured amorphously. One moment of experience could be chosen arbitrarily where from things could be looked back or forward to. The reader is guided straight into the protagonist's mind to live that chosen moment and is compelled to see life from that point as the protagonist himself.

Alan Moore says, 'Artists use lies to tell the truth. Yes ,I created a lie. But because you believed it, you found something true about yourself.' Observed in this perspective a story could be for some the subjectivizing of a truth told as a tale, or an objectification of lies that could be presented as truth. And so, every life is a story, and every individual lives the truth and the lie of that story. Stories, when told with honest passion, can build up an eternity out of a single moment, or can shrink centuries into that one, single moment.

The stories in this collection make an effort to examine the manifold aspects of human behaviour that appears normal in normal circumstances but can change inexplicably under pressure exercised either by the society or the people around us or by an inconceivably intriguing inner conscious. While some of them set out to probe the subliminal, to uncover the truth deeply embedded there that all tales of human existence are woven around, to define the terrible conflicts our souls are torn with, some others try to capture the varying moods of man caught in a web of prejudices and predilections, ambitions, fantasy, and vain pursuits. There are stories that try to portray men and women as pathetic victims of social injustice, poverty, superstition and a malignant destiny. They are tales of suffering and sacrifice of men and women, of the harsh disillusionment that spring from unfulfilled desires. In a way they too are attempts to define the weird and mysterious acts of the characters, whether an adult or a child, through an exploring of the many layered and obscure pattern of man's subconscious.

We all know that a story can be told in several ways. In the words of Khalid Hosseini 'A story is like a moving train: no matter where you hop on board, you are bound to reach your destination sooner or later.' These stories too, irrespective of the manner in which they are told, intend to create what Poe calls the "single effect" to guide the readers to the right destination. The response of the readers, hence, would decide the extent of their success in accomplishing the goal.

Snehaprava Das

Night of the Snake

Damaru Lakra watched his daughter, the youngest of the three, sleeping peacefully on the flax mat. Careful not to make a sound, he groped cautiously under the big wooden chest that stood against the opposite wall and pulled out the sack. He swathed his hands with some discarded clothes and sitting away from the sack unknotted the length of rope that was tied around its mouth. No sound came from inside the sack. He did not have the nerve to look inside. The room, however, was in darkness.

But, Bhola had given him his word, 'It is one of the deadliest'. He had assured Damaru. He cast a last look at the sleeping girl and sneaked out of the room. He closed the door behind him noiselessly and walked up to the extreme end of the veranda. He felt faint and slumped on the clay floor. Tears streamed down his eyes and a hard unreleased sob threatened to choke him. With a heart that pounded violently he waited for the inevitable scream of his eight-year old daughter.

Damaru had made up his mind several months before, in another wet night like this. He had a family of five to feed and just a small patch of farmland on the lower slope of the hills. He grew ragi and maize and sweet potatoes there. But even after bone breaking toil the land yielded not much to meet the expenses of even the bare minimum requirement of the family. Survival had become a cruel joke. His wife and three daughters went to the jungle to collect wild nuts and fruits and firewood. Most of the days they had to manage with gruel and wild fruits. Hardly, with any luck if he could manage to sell the frugal quantity of ragi , maize or sweet potatoes in the marketplace, the family ate rice and potato curry. There were times when he and his wife had to go without food for days. With no money, no food, no proper clothes, life was a living hell.

The idea had struck him when a snake bit the son of Tabita Lakra sometime before.

It rained hard that night. Water had come inside most of the huts in the village. Damaru slept in the dingy room where the chest was and his wife and three daughters slept in the space adjacent to it that served as the kitchen. Water dripped from the broken thatch and the kids squirmed into the tattered rag in a vain effort to keep themselves dry.

A loud howl from the hut of Tabita Lakra jolted him out of an uneasy sleep.

The shrill cry was followed by a loud uproar. Damaru sprang off the mat he was lying and putting on his straw head-cover he hastened to Tabita's hut. A crowd had gathered outside the hut. Tabita was crying beating his chest. A woman, perhaps Tabita's wife, wailed inside the hut. Outside, people chattered loudly, everyone raising his or her voice in an attempt to be heard above others and no one succeeding in making it intelligible. All Damaru could make out was 'Buchhan' and 'Snake'. Buchhan was Tabita's twelve-year -old son. His heart hammering, Damaru pushed through the crowd and ran up to Tabita.

Tabita howled loudly at the sight of Damaru. 'My son... my son...' he cried bitterly, Damaru looked inside. Buchhan lay on the soaked mud floor. His face was swollen and looked bluish and patchy. His hands and legs had gone stiff. Foam drooled out from one corner of his mouth. There was no doubt that the boy was bitten by a snake.

Just at that moment Nitu, the young son of Sambaru Lakra arrived with the witch-doctor. Nitu lifted the boy and brought him out to the front of the hut. He laid him down on the ground. The crowd formed a circle as the witch-doctor began the act of neutralizing the snake's poison. He hopped around the boy brandishing a stick in the air. A bunch of peacock plumes were fixed to one end of the stick. The face of the witch-doctor wore an ancientness that was as black as the dark night. The thick, unkempt mass of copper coloured hair were tied in a ponytail at the back of his head. There were several strings of different coloured beads around his neck that rattled and clattered to the tune of the weird sounding mantras he droned as he hopped around the unconscious boy. The crowd watched wide eyed. Buchhan's father and mother and two sisters gaped at the wild antics the witch-doctor performed waiting with bated breath for the signs of life returning to the boy's still body.

Nearly a quarter of an hour passed. Nothing happened. There was no stirring, not even the slightest, in Buchhan's body.

The witch-doctor chanted the mantra more loudly and danced more wildly. His eyes glowed like tiny beads of red. Still, there was no movement in the stiff body of the boy.

And then, Rajula arrived at the spot.

'Stop all this nuisance. Let's take him to the hospital.' He shouted angrily. The witch-doctor was out of his mind in anger.

'Do not interrupt, you ignorant young man', he snarled at Rajula. 'The mantra will not work.'

But Rajula did not wait. He was an educated boy. He had studied in the school in the nearby town. Not caring for the darkness and the rain, he and some of his friends lifted the boy to a stretcher made of bamboo poles and rags and carried him along to the government hospital in the town.

Buchhan's father, Damaru and some other men ran after them.

The witch-doctor pronounced an ugly curse on the villagers and stormed away from the place.

It was after midnight when they reached the hospital. The boy was carried inside by a couple of attendants.

A sleepy nurse took a look at the boy. 'A snake bite case?' She asked indifferently.

'Yes sister, please save him,' Rajula said politely.

'I will give him the antivenom injection. But you will have to wait till the doctor comes in the morning.'

'Please do something. Send a message to the doctor. I am afraid it will be too late if we wait till morning', Rajula urged as the nurse loaded the syringe and pushed the needle into the boy's stiff arm.

She looked up at Rajula.

'I think you are already too late.' She said.

Rajula looked helplessly at her.

'Please do something'.

'I have done what I could do in this situation. I think the boy was dead before reaching here. But the doctor has to confirm it. He will write the death certificate. In any case you have to wait to get the body. A post mortem has to be done to ascertain the cause of death.'

'But we won't want our child's body to be cut and torn,' Damaru interjected.

'Won't you?' The nurse said. 'Then how are you going to claim the compensation amount?'

'What compensation?' Rajula looked at the nurse in surprise.

'Our government gives compensation for snake-bite deaths. Don't you know that?'

Rajula and Damaru looked at each other.

'How much?'

'Depends...two or three lakh perhaps. I am not sure.'

'Three lakh!!' Damaru stammered... Three lakh is a fortune!!' He rushed outside where Tabita and others waited.

'The boy is probably dead.' He blurted out.

Tabita let out a wild scream.

'But the doctor needs to confirm the cause of death. It can be done only when they cut open the body and examine. Then you will get an amount of two or three lakh as compensation.'

The wild screams stopped abruptly.

'What is that again?'

'You will get a compensation of three lakh rupees if it is confirmed that Buchhan died of snakebite.'

Shoving aside Damaru , Tabita strode inside. The nurse and Rajula stood by the body of Buchhan. They looked at Tabita in surprise.

Ignoring the puzzled look in their eyes Tabita asked:

'Will I be getting three lakh rupees if the doctor says that my son has died of snakebite?'

'Of course, you will. But the doctor would need proof. A post mortem, therefore, is a must. All of you wait outside.' The nurse motioned them to go out and dismissed the subject.

The doctor who stayed in the vicinity arrived at dawn break. He inquired about the incident and the nurse told him.

'We have to wait for the post mortem report he said to Rajula. Let the forensic pathologist who will do the post mortem come.'

The body of the boy was moved to the mortuary.

It was nine o clock in the morning when the other doctors and nurses arrived.

By the time the post-mortem was completed it was late afternoon. They brought back the body and got it cremated.

Damaru returned to his hut. It was evening. His wife Kanima was cooking millet stew in a clay pot on the earthen stove. On the veranda sitting around the kerosene lamp his three daughters were yelling at one another to prove their individual right over a bowl of puffed rice. Their loud cry and squeals had transformed the veranda to a mini battlefield. Damaru's head ached. He drank a bowlful water in one breath and slumped on the veranda. Kanima came to him. 'Poor Buchhan! What sin had he committed to rouse the anger of the Cobra-God?' She sighed and sat down by Damaru.

'Buchhan's death has become a blessing in disguise for his family!' Damaru said, looking into the precipitating darkness.

'What does that mean?'

'Do you know the government would pay Tabita an ex-gratia of rupees three lakhs?'

'Three lakhs?' Kanima's mouth hung open.

'Yes, three lakhs. Tabita could get his hut strongly thatched, could buy some pigs and hens, and good clothes for his children. He could keep some of the amount in a bank and earn interest on it. His life will be changed.'

'But Buchhan is gone forever.' Kanima sighed again.

'He has another son,' Damaru said. Tabita can send him to a good school in the town like the townspeople do. Three lakhs rupees is quite a sum. It will change his life.'

'Yes. Three lakh means a strong thatched roof overhead, hot rice and pulses two times a day, even tea in the morning and afternoon. It means good clothes and footwear for the kids. It means a lot many things,' Kanima thought.

Damaru kept turning on his sides all through the night. Sleep was miles away from his eyes. He could not decide whether to pity Tabita for the loss of his son or to envy him for the compensation money he was going to be paid.

'Why did the cobra choose Tabita's house,' Damaru asked himself, it could have chosen any other hut, even Damaru's !!

'Curse me!' Damaru reproached himself and fought the thought off. But it kept returning to his mind again and again. Finally, a little before dawn, he drifted into an uneasy sleep.

A couple of months passed. The village had forgotten Buchhan. His father and mother too had got over their loss. Tabita built another small room and got the living space extended. He had re-done the thatching and repaired the walls. His life has changed in many ways.

More months passed.

Damaru's life had remained unchanged. Hunger and hardship continued to torment him as they had been doing all the time.

Damaru was climbing down the slope of the hill after a day's hard labour when he chanced upon a man trudging ahead of him carrying a sack. The mouth of the sack was tied tightly with a length of rope. The man heard the footfalls of Damaru and looked behind. In the fading glow of the departing twilight the lean, haggard face looked familiar to Damaru.

He was Bhola, the snake charmer who lived with his family at the outskirts of the village.

'Aren't you Bhola?' Damaru asked.

Bhola's creased face lit up with a smile.

'Right. And you are Damaru , isn't it?'

'Yes. What are you doing here?'

'I had gone to the jungle beyond the hills. I often go there to catch snakes.'

'Oh! '.Damaru nodded. ' Did you get some of them?'

'Only one. But brother, what an animal it is!! A pit viper, one of the most poisonous species. Its venom will fetch quite an amount.'

'The snake is in there?' Damaru asked pointing at the sack.

'Sure. It is there.' Bhola announced smiling with the pride of someone who has won a difficult battle.

'It was trying to dodge me first. One small slip and I 'd have been lying dead in the jungle. But I have a lot of experience in handling these babies. Finally, I won and imprisoned it in the sack.'

'Do you catch cobras too?'

'Lots of them. They too fetch good money. The hospital people buy them. I do not know exactly what they do with them, but I guess they collect the venom from these snakes and sell it to some pharmaceutical company or something for making life saving drugs.'

'Snakes could be lifesavers!! Unbelievable!! Damaru was thoroughly puzzled.

'But yes, they could be, in a way. Snakes could take one life and save many if the government pays three lakhs of rupees to the family of the deceased,' he reasoned.

Anyone who is ready to sacrifice one of the family members can get the amount. But it is a tough choice. Every loved one's life is priceless.

Damaru lay on the flax mat and thought about

Bhola. What a man! Imagine facing a deadly snake alone! His thoughts travelled to Tabita and poor Buchhan. The boy had sacrificed his life to haul Tabita's life out of the bottomless pit of poverty and misery. Can a miracle happen to lift Damaru out of the dark depth he was stuck in?

Damaru wrestled with the thought but it was too strong, too domineering to be overpowered by the feeble defences of Damaru's conscience.

Night after night the disturbing thought kept coming back to him, driving sleep away till it became an obsession.

What must he do?

Damaru looked around as he walked down the slope of the hill. He was not sure if he really wanted to meet Bhola. The wish was there, suppressed and dormant like a snake lying innate, overpowered by the snake charmer's magic herb. He did not know what he wanted from the snake charmer, but there was something inside him, a fierce goading which he could not resist.

It was a fortnight since he had last seen Bhola with his snake-sack. May be, he was collecting snakes in some other jungle. He might not come into sight again for months, Damaru thought and quickened his pace.

It was, as Damaru had thought, nearly two months before he came across Bhola at the foothills.

It was much late in the evening. A halfmoon was struggling through thick patches of clouds. Damaru and Bhola emerged from the jungle. They stood talking in a hushed voice for a moment, and walked away in different directions.

Lying on the mat Damaru stared at the thatch. Night hung like streamers of black from the bamboo-rafters. His gaze travelled around the room. The tail-end of a tattered sari of his wife dangled from the clothesline. He closed his eyes and the sari became the long, crooked length of a snake. Damaru opened his mouth to scream but no sound came out. He tried to run away but his hands and legs had gone stiff. The dark creature descended upon him and coiled around him like a cold rope, tightening its grip at every twist. His breath came out in strangled gasps. He was bathed in sweat.

A hand shook him. Damaru opened his eyes and looked at the worried face of Kanima..

'What is the matter with you?' She asked in concern.

Sunlight was streaming in through the wooden bar of the small window. He turned his eyes to the clothesline. The sari was not there. Kanima has changed into it after taking her bath.

He squinted into the bright sunshine that slanted on the veranda and stretched off it to reach the edge of the thickets. He could see his two elder daughters in nicely fitted school uniforms hopping down the veranda. He turned his gaze towards his wife, she wore a silk saree with a floral print and a wide red border. A pair of gold eardrops dangled from her ears. She looked beautiful. He got up and ran outside. 'Whose house is this? He was puzzled. The house wore a new and transformed look with its strongly thatched roof and cement-plastered brick walls. The aroma of freshly cooked fish curry drifted out of the house through the newly painted windows. He took in a deep breath and smiled happily.

'What is wrong with you? Why are you smiling like this?' Kanima shook him hard.

Damaru opened his eye wide and looked at Kanimma.

Was he dreaming again, in the broad daylight? He wondered. But it was a different dream. It was neither scary nor gloomy. He felt relaxed and light hearted.

'Nothing. Just a dream.' He said.

Damaru went to the village marketplace to sell some ragi and sweet potatoes. The day proved to be a lucky one. All the sweet potatoes and ragi were sold within a short time. He bought a kilogram of rice, a little cooking oil, half a kilogram of potatoes and some tomatoes and spices with the money he got. He handed the bag of rice to his wife, Kanima. 'We will eat hot rice tonight,' he said. 'The millet and the sweet potatoes were sold for a good price. Cook the potatoes along with the tomatoes in a spicy gravy to go with the rice. The girls have not eaten potato curry since a long time.'

A grey and beige twilight sprawled over the hills. Bhola, carrying a sack with its mouth tightly tied with a string walked up to the tree where Damaru stood waiting. There was not a single soul in sight. The sack exchanged hands.

'Do not forget your promise. Two thousand......'

'I have given my word. But you have to wait till I get the money...'

Bhola touched Damaru's arm. 'Be careful. It is dangerous.' He walked away.

Damaru waited for the evening to deepen. He

returned when the night birds began to hoot and chatter invading the silence of the forest.

Careful to keep out of sight of any curious neighbour he ran into the hut and shoved the sack under the wooden chest. He heaved out a deep breath.

'Food is ready. Come and eat.' Kanima announced.

The three girls ran into the kitchen space and sat down, nudging one another as they did so. 'I am very hungry, Ma,' Eight-year-old Sina, the youngest of the girls, said.

'We are too,' the elder sisters cut in. Damaru picked Sina to his lap. 'You eat with me tonight,' he said fondly, cuddling his daughter. Kanima placed the banana leaves in front of Damaru and the girls. She dished out hot rice on the leaves. She ladled the potto curry out of the steaming pot and poured the curry on the rice. Damaru made a ball of rice mixed with the curry and put it into Sina's mouth. 'Eat as much rice and curry as you like.' His voice choked. He could not speak another word. His eyes burned with tears that were frozen.

The girls ate their fill of rice and curry, and prepared for sleep. Outside, the night was getting thicker.

Damaru was desperately trying to think of a pretext to get the youngest one, Sina, to sleep in the small room where the wooden chest was kept.

'Father, can I sleep in this small room tonight?' Sina said as if she could guess her father's mind.

Damaru looked sharply at his daughter. He lifted her up in his arms and kissed her forehead.

'Don't, Damaru, don't!! ' A voice screamed in his

ears. His head began to spin. He looked up at the black, swollen sky.

'Tonight it will rain again,' he thought, rubbed his eyes that burnt with unshed tears and put the girl on the flax mat and lay down beside her.

Thunder crashed outside. Damaru sat up on the bed. He cast a long look at the sleeping girl and crawled to the wooden chest. He pulled out the sack. He could feel the laboured twist of the hard rope-like thing inside. He bandaged his hands with clothes and untied the mouth of the sack, and stole out of the room.

A lightning flashed. The room was lit up for a brief second and then plunged into darkness.

Damaru walked up to the end of the veranda and slumped on the earthen floor. Thunder crashed again. Then it began to rain....... Torrents of liquid spikes hurtled down piercing the air. A lassitude swept over him He closed his eyes and waited for the inevitable scream.

*****

A Fairy Tale

A big full moon shone in the cloudless sky like a round plate of silver. Above it a few stars blinked sleepily at one another. Down below, the river was a ribbon of sparkling blue. The ripples curled passionately when the cool breeze wafted over them.

The fairy looked at the earth below. She loved to roam about the moon washed forests. So, she came floating down waving her fairy wings, her frilly white mantle billowing in the fragrant wind.

She landed by the river and sat down. The river sang sweetly to her and the gentle breeze caressed the flounces of her gown. She sat for a long time listening to the river-song.

Then she dozed off.

A small sound that was somewhat a mix-up of a whimper and a moan brought her awake. She pricked her ears and tried to listen while her curious gaze travelled around to detect the source of the sound.

It came from a nearby thicket to her left. The fairy rose and wandered to the thicket. She looked closely at a tiny white bundle that lay on a partially shaded patch. The soft whimper was heard again, now more clear and more exact. It came from the tiny bundle. The fairy sat down beside it and tried to see inside. A new born baby, swathed in white clothes moaned beating its tiny arms and legs as if complaining of the discomfort and hunger. The fairy picked up the baby fondly and held it in her arms. The baby stopped whimpering as if it could sense that it was in safe hands.

The fairy took off the white cloth the baby was tucked in. It was a baby girl, lovely and pink like a fresh bloom of rose. The fairy waved her magic wand. The trees bent down their branches and made a small leaf- cottage for her. The thick grass made a soft carpet of green. The fairy walked into the leaf hut carrying the baby girl in her arms. She waved her magic wand again and a silver bowl full of milk appeared instantly. She fed the baby girl milk with a silver spoon.

The baby smiled at her, the fairy smiled at the baby and the moon smiled at them.

The fairy made a baby bed with tender leaves and put the baby in it and sang a lullaby. The baby went to sleep and dreamt of the fairy. The fairy did not return to the fairyland above and stayed back.

She waved her magic wand and turned the modest leaf-hut to a big wooden house. She grew many flowering plants in the large patch of land in front of the house. There were roses of all colours, chrysanthemums, cannas, and jasmines. The fairy tended them with love and they grew lovely flowers. A big, bushy jasmine plant that grew large flowers was her most favourite. The jasmines looked bright and shone like silver sequins in the moonlight.

She named the baby Jasmine-Joy.

Seasons came and went. Days and nights rolled into months and months to years. Jasmine-Joy grew up under the care of her fairy mother to become a beautiful young woman. The fairy trained her in singing and dancing. The girl sang like a nightingale and danced like a sprite. She looked like a wingless fairy. The fairy never let Jasmine-Joy out of her sight fearing that some wild animal might bring harm to her.

Jasmine-Joy sang with the birds, danced by the river and slept tucked in the white mantle of her fairy mother.

She woke up to the bird song, swam in the river, sprinted after the deer. She loved when sunlight filtered through the dense foliage of the trees and made patterns on the forest floor. She danced to the rain rhythm, sang under the magic shadow of the floating moonbeam. When the fairy watched her dancing and heard her singing, she was overwhelmed with a strange rapture. She decked the girl with floral tiara, floral armlets and bracelets, and floral hair bands.

'Mother what is there beyond our forest?'

Jasmine-Joy asked as they sat together on the moonlit river bank.

'There are big cities and villages out there. There are big concrete buildings and motor- run vehicles. The automobiles rush along wide asphalt roads making a loud noise. '

'Who live in those buildings? Who travel in the automobiles?'

Humans like you live in the huge buildings. There

are small houses too. Some humans live in those houses because they are poor.'

'What is poor, mother?'

'Because they do not have enough money to buy good food or good clothes.'

'We are living in this wooden house. We eat only what we get in this forest. We do not have that thing called 'money ' with which humans get good food and good clothes and good houses. Are we poor, mother?'

'We are happy, even if we do not have money. We are not poor because Nature has provided us all we need to live. Are you not happy?'

'Very!' Jasmine-Joy said. 'But I want to see the city. I want to see how humans live in the big concrete buildings and ride motor run vehicles. Mother, can I go to the city? I will come back as soon as possible, ' Jasmine-Joy asked.

'No.' The fairy said firmly. ' Cities are dangerous places, and the humans are dangerous too. I can't put you at risk. '

'I will not be gone for long. I will hide myself somewhere safe and see the humans, the buildings, the streets and the automobiles. Please mother... just for a little while.'

Jasmine-Joy implored.

There was such a deep yearning in her big eloquent eyes that the fairy could not refuse.

'But make sure to come back before it gets dark. ' The fairy said, a strange premonition gnawing at her heart.

'I will mother. Don't you worry.'

Jasmine-Joy hugged her fairy mother, kissed her and sprinted away towards the edge of the forest. The fairy stood watching at the departing figure. She stood there in the garden a long time after Jasmine-Joy disappeared. She touched the big satin blooms of jasmine fondly. She came out of the garden but did not go inside the big wooden house. She sat on a wooden bench on the porch of the house and waited for Jasmine-Joy.

The afternoon sun dragged itself slowly to the west. The loud chirpings of birds filled the sky as they flew back to their nests. The fairy was a bit worried. There was no sign of Jasmine-Joy. The sun took a plunge down. The fading crimson in the west melted into the grey-black of the approaching evening. Soon it would be dark.

The fairy went in and lit the candles in the tall silver candle stand.

She was getting impatient.

Where was Jasmine-Joy?

The fairy came out to stand by the gate. She stood there for some time looking at the narrow winding path that disappeared into the forest. Then she came back and paced about the garden restlessly.

A strong wind began to blow. Would there be a storm? The fairy's heart began to beat hard. She was sick with fear.

What had happened to the girl?

Had she lost her way?

Had she been harmed?

The wind whistled through the trees. Crooked

lightning flashed continuously ripping apart the darkness of the evening. The thunder crashed with a vengeful violence.

A gust of wind blew past the jasmine bush and the plant drooped helplessly in the slashing rain. The wind tore at the flowers and shoved them down to the ground. The fairy stared fearfully at the big white flowers. In the flitting light of the lightning something caught her eye.

A thin red line .....

......flowing slowly from under the bush. She moved closer and squinted at it. Her startled hand pressed her mouth tightly to kill the scream that was about to escape.

It was not a flowing red line!

It was blood!!

The jasmines were scratched all over and smeared in red. Her heart at her mouth the fairy peered into the darkness. The rain had slowed down. The thunder was a distant rumble. The lightning too had lost its force.

Suddenly she saw a white figure in a distance. It was moving towards the house. The fairy ran out of the garden.

Yes, it was Jasmine-Joy!!

She lurched towards the gate. The fairy feared that the girl might fall any moment and ran towards her stretching out her arms. But Jasmine-Joy wailed loudly and pushing the fairy aside ran into the house. In the faint after-storm-light the fairy saw that the girl's windblown hair was smeared with dirt and dust. There were unmistakable blood stains on the flouncy white gown. A thin scream escaped the fairy.

Jasmine-Joy entered the house and shut the heavy wooden doors behind her with a bang. The fairy rapped frantically at the door.

'Open up darling!' She cried.

'Let me in. I will set everything right. Don't you worry at all my child!!'

But Jasmine-Joy did not open the door nor did she give any answer.

The fairy slumped on the wooden bench on the porch. She shut her eyes and prayed and waited for Jasmine-Joy's agitated mind to calm down a bit.

She smelt the smoke before she could see it. Thick clouds of black smoke were swirling out through the windows and from under the door. Then almost at the same moment she saw the ugly curls of fire and felt the heat.

Her heart gave a somersault and she screamed out loudly beating at the door with all her strength. She perhaps could have got the fire put out with her fairy power but her magic wand was inside the house. In a frenzy of terror, she ran around the house to find out some way to save Jasmine-Joy. She could hear her muffled screams amidst the loud hiss and crackle. Her mantle caught fire and soon she was engulfed in the flames. She flapped her fairy wings and climbed up into the air. Below her the big house was an enormous blaze of red and orange and yellow.

The fairy tried to move faster, but her wings too had caught fire. The burning crumples of her white mantle and gown drifted in the air. She tried hard to soar up but her broken and half burnt wings made it almost impossible.

The fairy swayed in the air like a flaming silver bird for some time and then disappeared in the vast emptiness between the earth and the sky.

Next morning a rain-washed sun shone on the huge debris of the house. Nothing was left of it. The garden with all its roses and jasmines and chrysanthemums had become a huge heap of black ash.

Below the debris something glittered in the early sunlight.

It was the half-melted silver magic wand of the fairy.

*****

A House for the Doll

She could feel the movement. It was very light, almost negligible as if someone was gently pulling the chair she sat on. She stood up and looked around. She was in her study room upstairs. Though sparsely furnished the room was comfortable and cosy. There was a big study table on which there was a laptop, and a chair. A single bed, a small, cushioned bench, a wardrobe and a book rack completed the furniture set up. Her doll, in her glitzy red gown sat in a neatly carved niche on the wall. She had other playthings, too. But the doll was special. She would never let it out of her sight. Her father had got the niche specially designed for the special doll.

It was early evening and she had come upstairs to study after saying her prayers. She sat down again and opened her notebook. The chair shook immediately as she did so. She stood up, disturbed by the movement, and looked around. Everything was in place. She sat down.

She sensed it again.

This time the movement was more clear and more well-defined. She sprang up from the chair as the ceiling fan began to sway. The books fell on the floor in random scatters. Even as she turned to look at it, scared out of her wits, the doll took a headlong dive to the floor. She picked up the doll hurriedly.

And the lights went out.

Screaming, she stumbled down the steps that led to downstairs. She ran into her mother's arms who was coming out of the kitchen, bewildered. Mother sat down holding her in her arms. She buried her face in her mother's lap, shutting her eyes tightly. 'Do not fear, dear,' her mother said. 'It is a mild tremor and will soon pass', she added to comfort her. But she did not open her eyes and kept pressed her face hard into her mother's lap.

++++++

She lay on the wet floor, her face buried in her mother's bosom, gripping the doll tightly.

'Do not panic my darling, the storm will pass soon,' mother repeated. 'Keep praying, ' she added and mumbled her prayers. The storm howled like a monster gone mad. The thatch of the room in which they sat clutching and grabbing each other was blown away and floated in the air like an ugly mass of grey cotton wool before breaking into pieces. She screamed wildly as the heavy rafter came blundering down on them.

The weather was fine in the morning. The morning was bright and slightly warm. The leaves in the big acacia and fig trees fluttered in the comforting breeze blowing from the south. She and Jhuma played with the doll in the backyard of her house. The doll was an amazement. It was dressed in a bright red gown. Its hair flowed in silky tresses around its chubby face. The most beautiful thing about the doll were its blue eyes which closed and opened when it moved its head. The eyes got shut if it was laid down in a sleeping position, and opened when it sat up. It looked like a tiny, live girl. She had been asking her father to get her a doll like that since many months. Father said he would bring one when he went to town to sell the farm produce. At last, after a long wait her wish was fulfilled. She was more than happy.

Mother called out to her. 'Won't you eat your midday meal today? Come and take bath. Your father will be here soon. '

'We will play again in the afternoon. You go and eat your midday meal.' She said to Jhuma before she left for her home on the other lane.

Mother asked her to take a nap. 'Don't go out in the sun,' she warned. 'You will be punished if you do.'

She lay in the bed waiting for her mother to sleep. Slowly, careful not to make a sound, she slid off the bed when she heard her mother's light snoring. She picked up the doll that was lying on the bed by her side. Opening the door softly she tiptoed to the courtyard, unlatched the bamboo-screen gate and came out. She walked to Jhuma's house and called out her name. Jhuma came out immediately as if she was waiting for her call.

Let's play in the mango orchard.'

'Alright. Come!'

It suddenly became cloudy as they reached the mango orchard which was at a little distance from their house. The sun hid behind the thick patches of clouds that swam into the sky from nowhere.

'It may rain.'

Jhuma said looking at the sky. They could hear

the light rustle in the trees as they looked at the river at a distance.

Something like a black column rose spiralling from the water. The girls watched wide eyed, rooted to the place where they stood. Within seconds the black column of smoke grew huge and enormous and began to gyrate at an unbelievable speed. The girls ran back to their homes as fast as their legs could carry them. They saw people who worked in the fields running towards the village. In no time the village was wrapped in a blanket of black and it became impenetrably dark. She clutched at her mother with all her strength and began to scream.

'Where is your father?' Mother cried out and chanted a prayer, holding her tight. Father came running into the courtyard and the bamboo screen door of the courtyard went whirling up into the sky the next instant. The air was loud with the cries of the men and women and the howls of the animals. Hens and ducks were catapulted up into the air, drifted blindly for a moment flapping their wings and came crashing down. Even cats and dogs were blown away and were thrown down by the raging wind. The ear-splitting noise of the thunderclap, the rattle of massive trees careening down, and the monstrous roar of the wind turned the village to a bedlam. The thatches of houses flew in the air like torn patches of brown-grey sheets before they were swept away towards the river. The cows bellowed wildly, the dogs howled, and the birds screeched like crazy.

And then it began to rain.

Streams of water hurling down from a swollen sky like liquid splinters lashed at the remains of the houses with a savage delight.

Mother slumped down on the wet floor.

She pressed her head hard into her mother's lap and whimpered.

'Do not be scared, dear. The storm will pass soon.' She said and resumed her prayers.

'Mother Goddess!! Save us' she kept repeating like a litany.

She wondered where her father was. Perhaps he had gone to the cowshed at the back yard. Will the cowshed be there now? The wind must have blown it away. Where is father, then?' She wanted to call out to him, but her lips felt stiff.

She tried to raise her head, but her mother pressed herself on her small body as the rafter came hurtling down. She heard the shrill scream of mother before she blacked out.

She was still clutching at the doll when the ODRAF team rescued her from under the debris. The tornado had smashed the village beyond recognition. All the thatched houses were razed to the ground. Dead and injured bodies of humans and animals and birds that lay cluttered around were beginning to stink. She looked at her mother who lay still under the heavy rafter, her face reduced to a pulp. She winced and shut her eyes. Then she began to cry.....

Hard, choking sobs shook her small frail body.

They took her to the relief camp where many men, women and children who had lost their family members and were rendered homeless had taken shelter. Days later she was taken to the orphanage. There were many children of her age there. Some were older and some were younger than her.

They slept in one room on the floor, ate coarse rice and dal in the dining hall and washed their plates and bowls.

Some months passed.

She made a few friends in the orphanage. She missed Jhuma. She hadn't seen her since the day the storm came. But the doll was her best friend. She talked to the doll and cried cursing her own fate. Sometimes she played with other children, but she did not let anyone to play with her doll.

More month passed.

One night the matron came to their room before they went to bed. The matron asked them to get up early next morning.

'We are having visitors. All of you should take bath and dress up before they arrive.'

The visitors arrived in a cab. A good-looking, middle-aged man, and a woman of the same age with a smiling face and kind eyes got down from the cab. The matron welcomed them and guided them to the large visitor's hall where the children waited. She sat stiff cradling the doll in the crook of her arm, looking down. The matron introduced them to the visitors. Then the man and woman walked outside followed by the matron. They stood discussing something. The matron turned her gaze again and again to the bench where she sat clutching her doll. Then she nodded and the three of them came inside.

'Come to me my child!' The woman said softly,

stretching a hand towards her. She looked at the matron helplessly. The matron smiled and gestured her to go to the woman. She rose to her feet and walked to the woman. The woman took her in her arms. 'Would you like to come to our home with us to stay, my dear?' She asked affectionately and touched her face. I will get you toys and chocolates. You will also go to school and study.' She did not say a word, but she did not feel bad. In fact, she felt quite comfortable with the woman. She wished the woman would keep speaking to her nice and kind words for a long time. After an hour or so the man and the woman went away. She felt a bit sad when they left.

That night she dreamt of the woman. It was rather strange, she thought. She often dreamt of her mother and woke up in the middle of the night, moaning and tears rolling down her eyes. It was after months another person had visited her dream and she did not wake up whimpering and shedding tears. She was filled with a sort of happiness when she woke up in the morning. She wished the kindly woman to return and take her in her arms. She somehow felt safe there.

She sat looking through the window, waiting. The woman had said she would take her and her doll to her home. 'May be, she just said it for the sake of saying something and had actually no intention of taking her to her home,' she thought feeling disappointed.

It was a fortnight before they returned. The formalities were completed, and the matron asked her to accompany the man and the woman to their house. The woman smiled fondly when she saw her. She gathered up in her arms. ' Call me Ma,' she said and kissed her.

The children of the orphanage bade her goodbye

waving hands. The matron gifted her a new dress, 'You wear this dress, child.' She said, touching her head. Be happy,' she gave her blessings.

'Can I take my doll to your house, madam?' She asked guardedly. The woman gathered her up in her arms. 'I am your mother. Call me Ma,' she said and kissed her forehead.

+ + + + + + + + + + +

It was a palace compared to her small clay house by the riverside. She missed her parents a lot and cried in the nights. But Ma pulled her close to her and solaced her. And she got familiar with the new home and her new parents soon. Ma and Baba never made her feel that she was not their own child. They had put her in a school. She had her own room, nicely furnished with a small wardrobe, a bookshelf, a small, cushioned bench, a study table a chair and her own bed. But she slept with Ma most nights. And her doll sat ensconced in the neatly carved niche in the wall, smiling its chubby smile. Life was limping back to normal mode.

Everything went on well till the evening that shook the doll's house once again flinging it down from its cosy seat. She could hear voices outside. People had come out of their houses and were calling at one another.

'It must be another whirlwind,' she thought pressing her head harder into Ma's lap. 'What is she going to do if the roof comes crashing down!! It was as if that disastrous evening has returned and this time with a determination to destroy her house and her Ma and Baba. She sobbed inconsolably and her body trembled violently. After a few seconds everything was calm and quiet. There was no more sound and no more throbbing. Even the power was restored. Cautiously she raised her head to look. Ma was sitting still joining her palms, saying a prayer. The voices outside died away as people returned to their homes. Ma opened her eyes and looked around. ' Thank God! It is over!!'

The calling bell jangled. Ma got up and opened the front door. Father, breathless and worried sick strode in. 'Are you both ok? He asked anxiously. ' Don't worry, ' Ma replied soothingly. 'The tremor lasted for a few seconds only.'

'Yes, ' Father said, breathing a sigh of relief. Thank God! It could have been nasty.' He pulled his daughter into his arms.

That night she slept clinging to Ma. She had also put the doll in the bed close to her. 'God is not always cruel,' she thought as she said her prayers. 'Thank You God! You have not destroyed the doll's house this time!' She covered the doll with a small towel and caressed her face. Then she closed her eyes and drifted into a dreamless sleep.

******

The Blue Umbrella

Rishi entered the room eleven days after they had carried her away from there. Everything looked neat and carefully looked after. His mother always liked things to be kept in their appropriate places. There was not a single crease on the bedspread. The pillow covers too looked washed and perfectly fitted to the pillows.

His sister perhaps had kept the room in its right shape. The wooden idol of Lord Jagannath that stood on the top of the closet did not have a speck of dust on it. The mirror fitted to the door of the closet too was dusted and polished clean. The TV set, the writing table and the large bookcase neatly stacked with many titles of English and Hindi and Odia which his mother had either bought or collected ...everything looked perfect. The assortments of decorative pieces on the shelves looked the same as they used to look years ago.

Rishi looked at his father who lay on the armchair, looking sightlessly at the roof. His father who loved to talk and snapped at mother at the smallest slip she made, had suddenly become mute. The tastefully furnished room sagged under the load of a strange silence.

A blue cylindrical object lying at one edge of the top of the closet caught his eyes. Curious, he pulled it out carefully. An umbrella, that was perhaps bright blue once but now had gone patchy and faded, was kept neatly folded in its plastic cover.

He remembered the umbrella. It was the same one his mother used to carry in her handbag while going to office. She held it over his and his sister's head while they walked to the school which was some three hundred meters away from their home. During those days children usually did not go to school in the school bus or in their parents' car or on the bike of the father, like they do now. They mostly walked to the school. The relatively older boys rode bicycles. The umbrella served a double purpose. It protected him and his sister from rain when it rained and from the heat of the sun too. Mother never let them walk without the protective shade of the blue umbrella. The umbrella, like his mother always held its caring drape stretched over her children, anxious to keep all the trouble at bay.

He had forgotten the umbrella after leaving school. He studied higher secondary for two years in a local college and then left his hometown. Later he went out of state for doing a specialized course. Life had been so rushed that he did not find time to communicate much with his mother. Most of his conversations were with his father. His sister too got married in the meantime. Somehow, he shrank inside as he confessed to himself, he had begun to feel indifferent towards his mother, as if he had lost the need of her in his life. Father continued to snub mother as ineffectual and incompetent as he had been doing all through out, drowning mother's feeble protests with his loud counter arguments. Rishi and his sister too, had by that time had come to believe that their mother knew nothing much about outside world.

A laconic, self-contained person, mother never tried

to defend herself or explain things to the children whom she had given birth and reared up with utmost care.

She did not dress in the way sophisticated ladies did. She wore her hair in a long plait, did not apply make up to her face. Rishi could not remember a day when mother had draped herself in an expensive sari or did her hair in modern fashion. All put together, his mother to Rishi, was an outdated woman who loved to live in the past. The glamour of the institute where he did his specialized course had gone into his head. Whenever his mother wanted to pay a visit to the hostel, Rishi stopped her on several pretexts.

He remembered the convocation ceremony. Almost all the students had invited their parents. But Rishi had shied away from the thought. Father could have come but he was afraid that if father mentioned the convocation ceremony mother might want to accompany him.

So, he did not let them know about the ceremony. Later, mother had learnt about it from one of her colleagues whose son also studied in the same institute. 'Have you not told aunty about the convocation ceremony?' His friend asked.

'Why do you ask that?'

'She said she did not know about the function when my mother asked her why she didn't come,' his friend said.

'I told her. She might have forgotten it. You know she keeps too busy ...'

Rishi was preparing excuses to justify his fault as he travelled home in the holidays that followed the function.

But mother never mentioned it. She got busy in preparing the dishes he loved and taking all care to see that he spent his days at home in comfort and happiness. The day on which he returned to the institute his mother got up early in the morning, did the puja and made breakfast for him. She had packed snacks and sweets in plastic jars for him. On day of leaving home for the hostel, as he bade goodbye to her Rishi looked into his mother's eyes for a brief moment. There was something in them he could not describe but which made him feel guilty. It appeared as if she strove to push back words that were about to escape her defying all her resistance.

Thereafter whenever he met his mother, he found her strangely quiet. She never made him feel that she was trying to distant herself from him, but he could sense it and felt ill at ease in her presence. He got a job and was posted in another city. Mother came and arranged things in his new house. Both father and mother stayed there for a few days and then left. He too got married after a couple of years. Mother loved Sheila, his wife and cared for her in the same way she did for him.

Though not obvious but the distance between them somehow grew increasingly more after his marriage. Mother and father came to live with them after his son was born. They were very happy and spent most of their time with their grandson. Since he and his wife worked in a multinational company and had to leave home around eight in the morning mother had to take care of the household responsibilities. She had to look after the baby too which in itself was a fulltime job. Sometimes he felt guilty to burden his parents especially his mother with these responsibilities at that age, but he too had no alternative. May be mothers are, as his father often commented, are a 'taken for granted' lot.

If she felt overworked or weary mother never complained. She appeared to be really enjoying herself in the company of her grandson. His wife, however, was not too happy about the way mother cooked traditional dishes of Rishi's choice. Like all women she also had her dreams of pleasing her husband by cooking new items for him. But she had no choice, too. She had to depend on her parents-in-law for the safety and proper rearing up of her child. But she was dissatisfied with the new dispensation. Rishi realized that his wife disliked her mother-in-law's extra involvement in certain matters, especially her interest in cooking special dishes for her son and the rearing up of the baby. Mother liked to feed the baby the food which she used to feed her own children. But his wife was in favour of following the nutritionist's diet plan for the baby. Though she never expressed it Rishi could understand his wife's unspoken resentment. He also understood that it was his duty to keep his wife happy. He recollected how he had adopted an apparently discrete way for doing so.

'I have made coconut cutlets, your favourite', mother said, coming out of the kitchen. 'Taste this one...' she put one cutlet on the plate. Rishi and his wife were eating a quick breakfast. His wife cast a glance of disapproval at Rishi. Rishi picked up the cutlet and kept it aside on another plate. 'Pack them in my lunch box mother, ' he said, 'we will eat it during lunchtime.'

'I have packed them for both of you in your respective lunch boxes. This one is just for tasting.'

'We are getting late,' Rishi cut in. 'There is no time for tasting it. We will eat it with our lunch', he said and got up.

He knew he sounded rude, but he had no other

option. 'Mother would forget it. She never minds my words,' he thought to himself and left for the office.

He could not detect any sign of accusation on mother's face when he and his wife returned in the evening. Mother and father were playing and laughing with his son and looked happy. But Rishi could now recollect, mother had thereafter never urged him to eat any of her specialties. She would cook and serve but never ask to eat more as she had been doing since he was a small boy. Everything seemed to have become suddenly very formal. He had not taken note of it at that time. The memory of one after another such incidents like this, which he had not cared to take seriously at that time, came flooding back, drowning him in a deep sense of regret. After his son started going to school, mother and father returned to their hometown. A year or so after Rishi and his wife left India to settle abroad.

His father, who was used to touring places while he was in office, found it difficult to spend long hours at home. And he took his frustration and boredom out on mother. Mother too had retired but her retirement was not taken seriously as her doing a job. Rishi and his wife mostly communed with father. Mother only wanted to ensure that they were all happy and in good health.

She hardly discussed anything beyond that.

Perhaps, Rishi tried to reason now, father would have cut her short or snapped at her if she tried to prolong her conversation with her son.

Rishi could not remember any occasion since his childhood when his mother had countered his father. That might be the reason why he and his sister had got to ignore their mother's advice and suggestions and believed her to be thoroughly incompetent and useless as other family members did. Even after all these years it was father who dominated the conversation.

Now as he stood holding the umbrella neatly packed in its plastic cover, he realized why the woman who had spread out herself like an awning of love and protection over them became cocooned inside a closed world. She had ungrudgingly folded herself and squeezed into the cover of her self-rejection.

Rishi took the umbrella out of its cover switched it open. He held it over his head for a while and then folded it. He ran his hand over the cloth that had gathered the patina of time over it and then put it back inside its cover.

His wife was doing the packing. They would be leaving the next day. His sister would stay for some more time with father and make the necessary arrangements.

'What is this?' His wife asked, holding out the blue umbrella. 'Why have you put it here in this suitcase?'

'I will take it,' Rishi said grimly, 'pack it along with my clothes'.

'But...' His wife tried to say something but held her words back.

'I will take my mother with me ... she has always tried to keep me close to her but has always been cruelly defeated. From now on she will always be with me.' Rishi promised to himself as he wiped his eyes.

******

Moon in Mommy's Face

She was getting late for the school. There was a staff council meeting to discuss the preparation for the annual examination of different classes. Eva was in a hurry. She prepared a sandwich breakfast for her six-year-old son Anshu and warmed the milk. She looked at the table clock for the third time that sat with an annoying nonchalance on the top of the cupboard in the dining hall. On other days she went to her school after leaving Anshu at his school which was only a few hundred meters away from her house. Then Jamuna the babysitter-cum- cook, would bring him back home at twelve o'clock. She would give him a bath and feed him. But there was a problem now. Some renovation work was going on in Anshu' s class room. And the classes were dropped for a week. Eva had asked Jamuna to come a little early in the morning. But she had not turned up yet.

Where was she? She should have been here by now. Eva was getting worried. She tried her number on the mobile phone, but it said the number was switched off.

Jamuna was a plump, middle aged and an affectionate woman who took good care of the boy. Anshu too was very fond of her. Jamuna has never given her any cause to get angry or disappointed in her. In fact, Eva felt relaxed when Anshu was with Jamuna.

Eva's husband was a marketing manager in a private company and had to do a lot of travelling. Eva taught in an Upper Primary School. She had to discharge the duty of a responsible teacher and take care of the household affairs at the same time. The burden of the dual responsibility exercised a heavy pressure on her. But there was no other alternative. Jamuna was a godsend who relieved her from this difficult situation. Not only that she took good care of Anshu, but she helped Eva a lot in other matters like cleaning the house and keeping things in order. She could trust Jamuna with many of the household responsibilities without any hesitation.

Eva walked to the grill gate and looked out. There was no sign of Jamuna.

She came inside and looked at her son, trying to take a decision.

'Anshu, my baby,' she coaxed her son. 'Jamuna aunty is late today. But she must be on her way. Can you manage alone for a few minutes? I will lock the grill gate from outside and give you the key. Jamuna aunty has a key too. If by any chance she has forgotten the key, you give it to her, and she would open the grill gate. Mummy has to attend an important meeting in the school. Mummy would be back as soon as the meeting is over. Are you afraid to stay alone for a while, son?'

Little Anshu looked up from the sandwich plate and gave a broad smile to his mother. 'Why should I be afraid, mommy? I am a big boy now. You go to your school.'

Eva's eyes watered. She ran her fingers through her son's hair and muttering curses on Jamuna she tried her mobile number once again. 'The number you are trying to connect is currently switched off,' the mechanical voice repeated.

'Where the hell is she?'

There was no time to speculate things. She wiped Anshu's face, switched on the cartoon channel on the TV, slung her handbag over her shoulder and rushed out. She latched the gate and turned the key in the padlock. She pulled the padlock twice to be sure and gave the key to Anshu who stood behind the grill gate waving at her.

'Bye, Mommy'

Bye, son, be careful. Do not give the key to anyone except Jamuna aunty. I will be back as soon as possible.

Eva started off on her scooty.

Anshu came back to take his seat before the TV set leaving the front door open. He kept the key carefully by his side.

'He is not afraid', he assured himself. 'It is a question of a few minutes. Jamuna aunty would be here soon.'

But as time moved on, he began to feel a little uncomfortable. Why was Jamuna aunty taking so much time? Suddenly he felt irritated with the noises the cartoon characters were making. He got up and switched the TV off. The house was plunged into silence. Anshu sat quietly for some time on the sofa listening to the sound of the occasional vehicles that passed by bringing in a short relief. The house was situated away from the main road in a residential area and so there was not much traffic on the road. He walked to the front door and stood waiting for a motor vehicle to pass by. One motor bike vroomed past. Anshu kept standing by the door till the noise died away.

The silence returned, in rushing waves, now more intense, and heavier.

Then he heard it!

Tick.. tick ...tick...

Gentle, but persistent. What was the sound? A bird? Rat?

In the thick, oppressive silence the soft, constant tick-tick sounded like the ticking of a bomb. Summoning up his courage he walked in to discover the source of the sound. He saw it then. The tick-tick came from the table clock that was on the cupboard. He looked at the clock closely. The three luminous hands were moving following a steady pattern behind its glossy shiny glass surface. Anshu knew the clock was an expensive one. His grandfather had gifted it to his mother and mommy cherished it as something very close to her heart. She kept it on the top of the cupboard out of Anshu's reach. But the clock looked strange now.

Even as Anshu watched it, the clock seemed to assume a face, a weird looking face that was neither human nor animal. And it seemed to be teasing him. 'Stop me if you can....tick..tick...tick...stop me if you can ..tick..tick..'

With every ticking sound it made the clock seemed to be inching forward to the edge of the cupboard. Any moment now it could lunge at him, and its hands would take his throat in their sharp, biting clutch. Anshu turned his eyes around frantically in search of a stick to counter the attack. He ran to the utility space and picked up the broom. Holding the broom handle in the tight grip of his small hand he raised it and swept a blow at the clock. Down came the clock with a loud crash scattering smithereens of glass on the floor.

'What happened Anshu baba?'

Jamuna cried from the front door. She rushed into the dining space and took Anshu in her strong arms before he stepped on the broken pieces of glass. She carried him to the drawing room and put him on the sofa.

'Now sit here quietly and do not get down until I say so.'

She went back and cleaned the floor with meticulous care. After cleaning the place carefully, she returned to the drawing room and called Eva. ' I am so sorry Didi. I had some unexpected guests this morning. My phone too had some problem so I could not contact you. Nor could I receive your call. But I am here now. Anshu baba is all right but... ' She stopped and looked at the boy.

'But... but what? Any problem?'

'Not exactly. The clock is broken,'

' Broken..? The clock? How?'

Eva's anxious voice crackled from the speaker of the phone.

'Seems Anshu baba was trying to bring it down and it fell ..' Jamuna said haltingly.

'O my God! My father's gift! Anshu has become so unruly. Where is he now?'

'He is now studying.' Jamuna replied looking at Anshu who sat watching her, listening to the conversation.

'Ok . Let him have his lunch in time. I will be back by two O clock. Tell him that he would be punished if he did not behave,'

Eva said and cut the connection.

Anshu took his bath and ate his lunch which Jamuna had cooked without any complaint.

'Now be a good boy and go to sleep...Anshu baba. I will finish the cleaning up, and then come to you.'

Anshu lay quietly in the bed. Time and again his gaze travelled to the big silver framed photo of his father and mother that stood on the bedside table. His mother wore a big, sweet smile. Her face was round and fair .. like the moon. Anshu thought as she looked at the photo. Then her mother's face changed. It no longer looked like the moon. It resembled the face of the clock. 'Wait, I am coming. I will see that you are duly punished for the damage you have done. You have hurt me, destroyed me. I will not spare you.'

Anshu closed his eyes tightly.

A few minutes passed. He opened his eyes gingerly, taking utmost care as if the clock in his mother's face would pounce upon him the moment it saw him opening his eyes. He cast a guarded look at the photo. Mommy smiled at him from it. The clock is perhaps hiding somewhere behind the photo, stalking him, Anshu thought.

Jamuna came in after finishing the cleaning up of the kitchen, spread out a mat on the floor and lay down. Soon the sound of her gentle snoring filled the room. Mother would be arriving any time now. He had to escape or else she would punish him for breaking her favourite clock.

He slid off the bed, careful not to make any noise, walked up to the door and opened it. He went to the front veranda. Jamuna aunty had not put a lock on the grill gate. Anshu opened the gate and walked out into the scorching sun. The road was deserted. Motorbikes plied in ones and twos. He kept walking straight. Anshu was not much acquainted with the road because he had never come that far alone. But he was not afraid. He was only afraid of the clock, and the way it could persuade his mother to exact revenge on him. Somehow the clock and his mother seemed to be partners in a conspiracy to inflict pain upon him, Anshu thought bitterly. He had walked far away from home. His legs began to ache, and he was feeling terribly tired. His eyes searched an unfrequented solitary spot to sit down and rest. There was small temple that stood under a massive Banyan tree. The place was well shaded and cool. A stack of bricks that had formed a small wall stood by the tree. Anshu squeezed his small body into the narrow space between the trunk of the tree and the brick wall. He was sure that his mother or Jamuna aunty could not find him now. The soft breeze caressed his exhausted limbs. He closed his eyes and fell asleep. He slept for a long time. It was dark when he woke up. He was feeling hungry. A big round moon looked at him from a cloudless sky. The moon smiled at him. Anshu looked at the moon intently, and his heart skipped a beat. The clock, God knows how, had gone up to the sky and merged into the moon. The moon-clock jeered at him from above. 'You can't escape now,' it said and leaned out, ready to jump at him. Anshu snapped his eyes shut, pressed his ears with his hands and began to scream,

' NO....Don't hit me. I am sorry. Please, don't hit me. I will never touch you again. Forgive me for this one time!!

He was still screaming at the top of his voice when a frantic and dishevelled Eva followed by an equally dishevelled Jamuna, and the police inspector and two constables reached the spot. Eva, tears streaming down her eyes gathered him up and held him tight. She began to kiss her son all over. ' Anshu, my darling!! My baby...she kept mumbling amidst sobs.

Anshu opened his eyes and looked at his mother's tear washed face. The clock was not there. He saw the police inspector who was looking anxiously at him. He turned his eyes up to look at the moon. The moon smiled sweetly. The clock was not there, too. Perhaps the clock has got frightened of his mother and these policemen and had gone away for good. He sighed with relief and clung closer to his mother.

Once again, he looked at his mother's face. Yes, the clock was not there. Instead, the moon smiled at him from his mother's face. He buried his head in his mother's comforting lap and closed his eyes.

******

Who is that in the Mirror?

She felt the prick of the sunlight on her face and opened her eyes. Sunlight was everywhere, on the bed, on the study table, on the mirror and on the wardrobe. She lifted her groggy eyes towards the wall clock. It showed ten past nine. Today too she would be late for the office, she thought grimly. She had gone to bed early last night, but the dream had returned.

It was the same every time. A spacious hall, walls painted in plastic emulsion and a silver framed photo of a good-looking woman hanging on one of them. The looks of the woman resembled that of her mother. Mini wanted to take a close look at it but the wall on which the photo hung seemed to be moving further away as she walked towards it. Mini would move faster and when the photo was about within the distance of her reach, it would suddenly disappear, and a mirror would take its place. And just as Mini stretched her fingers to touch its polished glass the mirror would come down with a loud crash, sending shards of glass, each of them carrying a distorted reflection of Mini's confounded face, flying across the hall.

She woke up and then turned restlessly on her sides for a long time. She had finally drifted into an uneasy sleep long after midnight. She dragged herself out of the bed feeling lousy and walked into the washroom. After a quick bath she went to the kitchen to prepare some light breakfast. The kitchen looked all cleaned up and shiny. There was a plate, covered with another, and a glass of milk on the dining table. She touched the glass of milk. It felt warm. Then she lifted the cover from the plate and looked. There were two pieces of buttered toast and an apple on the plate. The toast too was warm to her touch. Everything looked so ordered and neat in the kitchen. Her puzzled glance wandered around the kitchen. Who must have done all this? She asked herself. Had the maid returned from her village? Her cook cum maid had gone to her village in Andhra Pradesh to attend a marriage. She was not supposed to come so soon. Had she sent some proxy to do the cooking and cleaning? That seemed to be the most reasonable explanation at that moment. She finished the toast and the apple and drank the milk in large gulps. Slinging the laptop over her shoulder she hurried out of the house and locked the front door. She scrambled out of the elevator and ran to the parking lot in the basement. She started the scooty and drove off. She hoped she could make it just in time before the boss reached the office. Her boss was a gentleman, but a hard taskmaster. He believed in making the maximum use of time and wanted his employees to be extra punctual. 'To get everything done in its right time is the key to success.' He would often remark. 'What matters most is how you time your schedule.'

She lived alone in a two bedroom-hall-kitchen fully furnished apartment house. The big floor to ceiling window opened to a spacious balcony from where she could have a nice view of the distant horizon. In the morning, the sun rose from behind the mountain ridge, and in the full moon nights a big amber moon popped up shyly from one corner.

It was incredibly lovely. She did not like much company. In fact, she loved to have the house to herself where she could live as she wished without any intrusion or interruption. That was the reason why she had not let any of her colleagues share the house with her. She knew it would have saved her half the rent amount, but she preferred privacy over the extra expenses. She had been accustomed to living alone since her childhood, after the death of her mother.

She shuddered at the memory of her mother. The sight of her frail body hanging limply from the ceiling fan had remained permanently stuck in her mind. She could see herself crouching in a corner of the room, her tongue too stiff to let out a sound, her eyes burning dry, her body trembling uncontrollably. An aunty who was their close neighbour had held her tightly in her arms and was trying to console her. She sat by the aunty looking emptily at the scene that was enacted before her in a slow motion. The policemen taking off her mother's body and lowering it to a stretcher and then the stretcher being carried out to the ambulance, her father arriving there looking pale and flustered, and the policemen asking him questions, the media fellows clicking their cameras nonstop and shoving the cordless mike towards the policemen and her father and the neighbours who had thronged in the compound of the house asking mindless questions.

She did not have an easy and carefree childhood as most of her friends had. There was not a single day when her parents had not had a fight. They fought over almost every small issue ranging from the taste of the tea to the colour of the door curtains... Sometimes the fight took an ugly turn. An outraged father slapping hard his wife and the wife's violent reaction… the obscene abuses, the smashing of the cutlery, and the loud banging of doors…. turning the house to a mini battleground. She failed to fathom the reason of such nasty fights, but the noise of the yelling and clangs and crashes made her feel dizzy. The one consoling thing about the fights was that they did not last long. Her father would invariably storm out of the house after such a scuffle and would return very late in the night.

He would straight go to his room and lock the door and would not come out until after she left for the school. It was not so with her mother. She would be a different person after father went out. She would take her daughter into her arms and weep a little and then both of them would sleep.

In the morning she would scuttle into the kitchen to prepare some snacks for her. By the time Mini came out of the washroom and changed into the school uniform the house would be all shipshape. Her mother had a fetish for disorderliness. She could not stand any form of disarrangement. Everything had to be kept in its right place. She was a good cook and made delicious dishes for her. 'God only knows why she turns out to be a total stranger, cruel and harsh, while she fought with father,' she thought. She felt so humiliated and unhappy when her school friends proudly introduced their parents to the teachers during the parent-teacher-meeting days. She had to make several excuses to explain the absence of her father. Only her mother came to the school for her admission and other such official matters. She shied away from her friends. What would she say when they would want to know about her father? The constant rows between her parents had drawn the curiosity of the neighbours and they too asked her why her parents fought so often. She had no answer either for the inquisitive friends or the people in the neighbourhood or for herself. She knew both her parents loved her in their own individual ways, but it was mother who took care of her. Father remained out of home most of the time and when he was at home, he sat alone watching television or smoking cigarettes in the terrace. He would just greet her with a small smile or a gentle pat on her back. Sometimes he brought her toys and chocolates. But he did not talk much with her, nor did he take any interest in her school and her studies. Mother was different. She cooked food for her, nursed her through sleepless nights when she fell sick, helped her in doing homework, pressed her school uniforms and took her for shopping in holidays. In fact, mother was an altogether different person when she was with her, loving, kind and caring---- not like the screaming, dishevelled woman she got transformed into during the ugly fights with father.

She had often seen her mother sitting alone, brooding, her face a mask of gloom. She would sit for hours her eyes fixed at some invisible point in the ceiling. There was an empty look in mother's eyes which she found difficult to bear. She wanted to hold her mother tight, to bury her head in her chest to blend into her and become one with her at that time. She wanted to feel her pain, to shed her tears.

++++

It rained hard that night. She had completed her homework and watched the television while her mother cooked dinner in the kitchen. Her parents had not had a fight that day and she thought that it was all well between them at least for tonight. She looked through the window, feeling happy that she would eat her dinner with father. She heard the familiar sound of her father's car pulling up in the porch. The doorbell rang soon after. She ran out to open the front door. Father came in wearing a grim face.

'I will get you a towel Papa', she said and ran inside.

'How was the school today, dear?', his father asked as he dried himself.

'Fine, Papa. There was an interclass debate competition today. I stood second.'

'Good! Where is your mother?'

'In the kitchen. She is cooking dinner. You change your clothes and have a wash, Papa. I will set the table for dinner,'

'OK dear.' Father said and went inside.

It was ten in the night by the time dinner was over. Mother and father did not exchange a single word during the dinner. How Mini wished them to talk lightly over the food as most parents do. But nothing like that happened. They ate the dinner in silence. Father pushed back his chair and got to his feet. She helped mother to clean up the table and the dishes. Then she went to bed. She was feeling very tired and was asleep as soon as she lay in the bed.

The loud sound of the exchange of heated words between her parents from the adjoining room jerked Mini out of a deep sleep. She sprang up on her bed. She went to the door, slowly opened it, and tried to listen. Her parents were shouting at each other. Though she could not understand clearly, but from the snatches of the tirades that reached her, she could make out just as much that they were about a separation or something like that. She tried to listen more intently.

'I cannot put up with you anymore. You have made my life hell,' She heard her father's voice.

'I know,' her mother snapped. 'It is all because of that whore in your office!'

'Hold your tongue!' Father thundered, or I will strangle you!'

'What else could you do, you wretched two-timer!' Mother screamed.

'I have spoken to my lawyer. He will come to meet you tomorrow. I want to get rid of you at the earliest,' his father shouted and stormed out of the room, slamming the door shut behind him.

A few minutes later Mini heard his car starting up.

She tiptoed into the room. Mother sat on the bed, her face flushing red. Mini walked up to the bed and sat by mother. She clasped Mini hard and began to weep. Dry, choking sobs raked her frail body.

'It is late. You will have to go to school in the morning. You must go to sleep now,' Mother said, wiping her tears. Mini lay down in the bed and soon drifted into sleep.

'Get up dear. Get ready for the school.'

Mini woke up to her mother's calling. As always mother had packed her lunch in the lunchbox and put it in the school bag. Mini, her toilet and brushing and bath done, sat down at the table and ate breakfast. She drank the milk without any objection that morning.

Mother came to the front door as Mini was about to leave. She looked at Mother. There was a strange look in mother's eyes. She took Mini in her arms and kissed her.

'I know you can manage things by yourself even if I am not there. You are a responsible child. You will be brave and strong. Do not be a loser like me!'

A few drops of tears trickled down her eyes as she said this. Mini's heart went out to her mother. She wondered why father despised her and why such a gentle woman like mother nurtured such abhorrence for her husband. The school bus sounded the horn. Mini strode out of the gate. She cast a brief glance back. Mother was still standing at the door waving at her. She did not want to leave her like that. Reluctantly she walked towards the school bus.

It was three in the afternoon. The school bus dropped Mini and left. She walked back home. She was feeling a bit restless all through the day. It was difficult to focus on her studies. The events of last night and her mother's tear washed face kept returning to her mind. And why did mother say that Mini could manage things on her own and that she should be brave and strong? She almost willed the final bell to ring earlier so she could run back to her mother.

A couple of elderly men who stood in the grocery store nearby flicked a strange glance at her and turned their face. She quickened her pace. The first thing that caught her eyes were the two police jeeps and an ambulance parked outside the compound of their house. A crowd had gathered and some of the people were talking to the policemen. She pushed the crowd and ran inside shoving aside the hands of a policewoman who tried to stop her. She saw her father talking to a policeman. He looked pale and drawn. She saw some men in white uniform taking out a stretcher from the ambulance and walking in.

'What has happened? Why the ambulance? Has mother fallen sick? She wanted badly to speak to her father, but he turned his eyes away from her. She ran into the bedroom, her heart hammering.

Some policemen were trying to lower the body of her mother that hung limply from the hook of the ceiling fan. As an aunty from the neighbourhood pulled her into her arms and held her tight. She tried to pull her away from the spot. But she stood there rooted to the floor.

As she looked on unblinkingly, the scene in front of her blurred and was enveloped in a blinding white. The whispers of the crowd outside and around turned to a deafening roar. She began to fall, down and down into an enormous black depth of total silence.

The story of her life thereafter was brief, though paradoxically each day was one of endless agony.

Her maternal uncle brought her to his house and a short while after she was put in a boarding school. She could manage to have a few friends there and her days slowly fell into a pattern. The matron was a kind-hearted lady who sympathized with her. On her return from the school Mini always found her text and notebooks kept in the shelf, her clothes neatly folded, and the bed made. Her heart was filled with gratitude for the kindly matron. On a Sunday she went to the matron to express her gratitude.

'Come in,' the matron said as Mini stood undecided by the door.

Mini walked guardedly up to the table behind which the matron sat reading some official papers.

'What is it?' she asked.

'I have come to thank you madam.'

'What for?' the matron asked, looking amused and surprised at the same time.

'For taking pain to keep my things in order.' Mini stammered.

'I am keeping your things in order? Who told you that?'

'I know madam, who else will do that for me?'

'But I haven't done anything like that. All of you are dear to me. But I have not personally taken care to keep your things in order as you say,' the matron looked even more surprised. Mini felt embarrassed. Perhaps she should not have come here to say thanks to this good lady. She won't admit it.' She took her leave politely and came back to her room. When her friend and roommate Shaila came back Mini told her about her meeting with the matron.

'Are you not mistaken about the matron doing the cleaning up for you?' Shaila asked. 'She never does things like that although she is very fond of us.'

'Then who is keeping my things so properly arranged? It is she! She is doing it without anyone's knowledge because she pities me, because I am parentless.'

Shaila looked thoughtful. 'May be. She is probably doing it when all the inmates are at the school.

The matter was dropped at that. But Mini's things were always arranged neatly all the years she remained in the boarding school.

She happened to be lucky as far as hostel life was concerned. She did her Bachelor in Technology in a renowned private college and stayed in the hostel. This time it was Jaya, her sweet spoken room mate who took over the charge of keeping Mini's things at their proper places. She would hang the mosquito net and tuck its frills under the edges of the bed while Mini fell asleep through her reading. There were times when Mini would find a glass of milk, covered by a lid waiting for her when she returned tired and hungry from her classes. On another time it was a piece of chocolate cake, Mini's favourite on a plate. But Jaya would not be there in the room in all such occasions.

'I don't know how to say my thanks to you Jaya, ' Mini said when she found Jaya alone. The other roommate Razia had gone to her hometown.

'What for?' Jaya raised a pair of surprised eyes.

'Don't feign ignorance, my dear! I know you are doing so much for me because you know what I have gone through in my life, and you sympathize with me for that. But I seriously feel indebted to you.'

'I do not know what all you are saying. What have I done for you to make you feel indebted?' Jaya looked confused.

'She won't admit anything.' Mini thought. 'She is so skilled at hiding her feelings.'

'You may decline it, but you are as kind and gentle as the matron in the boarding school. She also tried to help me remaining invisible.'

'I might have helped you a little at one time or other. You need not take that so seriously. You too have helped me when I needed it. Haven't you?' Jaya said trying to keep the conversation light-hearted.

'I will not compel her to say it if she tries to keep it private'.

She never broached the subject again. Days rolled by. They were all in their final year. IT Companies came for the campus recruitment. Most of them got jobs with a good package. Mini and Jaya too got good jobs. They were so happy. It was late in the night when they came to bed after celebrating their success. A smiling teddy bear looking furry and cuddly sat in Mini's bed holding a big Cadbury chocolate in its lap.

'Wow!! How sweet of you Jaya! This is the best gift you could have thought of. You know my mother used to gift me teddy bears and chocolates when I performed well in any test.'

'But I have not brought it.' Jaya said, looking puzzled.

'Oh!' Mini bit her tongue. She had forgotten that Jaya would not self-advertise.' I should not have embarrassed her, she thought. 'I am sorry Jaya, may be one of the guests of some friend of ours has forgotten it here.' She said apologetically. Jaya walked over to Mini and hugged her tightly. 'Mini, you are so sweet yourself that you think everyone is as sweet as you. Remain like that, dear. We have spent such a good time here together. I will never forget you. And we will always keep in touch.' Jaya's voice was wet and her eyes heavy. Tears trickled down Mini's eyes.

'Of course, Jaya. We will always remain in touch.'

She joined her job and came to settle in this big city. She had taken a two bedroom-hall-kitchen apartment but had not entertained the suggestion to share it with a friend or a colleague. She had spent many years in the students' hostels and longed for a little privacy. It was a fully furnished apartment. Mini had brought a few suitcases while she moved in here. Amongst her personal belongings there was one suitcase in which there were some saris. They belonged to her mother. The suitcase was the only thing she cherished as a memoir of her mother. All other things of the house were taken care of by her maternal uncle who had brought her with him after her mother's death. Mini did not even have a photo of her parents with her. She had dared not to ask her uncle if he had one. She had hired a maid cum cook, Kartikaa, a slightly plump, middle-aged woman who came in the morning to clean up and prepare the breakfast and lunch. She drove to the office on her scooty most of the days. Sometimes she hired a cab. The office cabs dropped her and her colleagues at their places when they worked till late in the evening. Mini liked the arrangement. After a long time peace and quietude had settled in her life. In her leisure hours, which were very rare, she would sit on the balcony, a cup of hot coffee in hand, watching the teeming crowd and the rushing automobiles down below on the roads, and gazing at the silent, distant horizon.

She loved to read books and always went to sleep carrying a book in her hand. But in the morning Mini would be sleeping cosily tucked in a soft quilt, inside the mosquito-net and the book back at its place in the wooden bookshelf. Must be Kartikaa, Mini thought. She must have come early in the morning and done the cleaning of her bedroom. Kartikaa was a woman of genial nature. She had grown genuinely fond of Mini in the short span of a couple of months.

But Kartikaa had taken leave for a week and gone to her village to attend a wedding. So, Mini wondered if she has sent a substitute to do the cooking and cleaning. She sat down at the dining table and took a bite of the toast. Then she heard the soft whirr of the washing machine. The new maid must have put the clothes in the machine and left. Mini wondered again why neither Kartikaa nor the other maid had told her anything about it. But there was no time to think about that. She decided she would hang the clothes to dry in the evening. She switched off the fan in the dining hall, latch-locked the front door and started off on her scooty.

She looked up at her apartment as she parked her scooty in the basement. She could she the lighted window. She remembered she had left no lights on while she left for the office. Who had switched them on? The maid was perhaps there in the house. She came out of the elevator, walked up to her flat and pressed the doorbell. No body opened the door. She pressed again. Still, no one answered or came to open the door. She could hear the bell ringing behind the door. How careless of the maid! She had gone away keeping the lights on. She unlocked the door with her key and entered. The flat looked spic and span. 'I must call Kartikaa and ask her about this,' she decided as she changed into a casual outfit. Her eyes went to the clothesline in the inner side balcony. All the washed clothes hung there neatly clipped. She felt pleased. 'Very meticulous at her work, whoever she may me...' she praised the unknown character. She went to bed early that night after eating a dinner of her choice. It was as if she has cooked it herself.

She called Kartikaa.

Despite the network disturbances she could reach her over phone. There was a lot of noise. All she could gather from the conversation that Kartika had not asked anyone to come to Mini's home to do the chores in her absence. Lines of puzzlement came up on her forehead as she disconnected the phone. Who, then must be doing all these works? She could find no acceptable answer to that. Though she was feeling tired she kept turning on her sides for a long time. Finally, she drifted into an uneasy sleep.

The next day was a repeat of the previous ones. The breakfast ready on the table, rooms broomed and mopped, and the furniture dusted. She felt a frisson of fear. Is there a spirit or something like that dwelling here? She fought off the thought as soon as it occurred. 'It is absurd,' she tried to convince herself. But she must find out the secret character. She would have to speak to someone about this.

That day as she sat in the office in her cubicle pondering over the unusual things happening in her house, Varun came in followed by Ria.

'What is the matter Mini?' Why do you look so disturbed?'

'There is something strange happening in my house.' And Mini spurted out all the details, the breakfast kept ready on the table, the clothes put in the washing machine and then hung to dry, the swept and mopped floors, dusted furniture, and the lights switched on …

'I think there is someone in the house… someone whom I am not able to see!'

'You mean … a ghost or something? Ria's hand went to her mouth. 'A friendly ghost, like they show in the movies and serials??' Her eyes bulged out.

'Cut the crap', Varun snapped. 'There is no such thing as a ghost. What I presume, someone has somehow got hold of the key. That someone has got a duplicate key made with which he or she enters your house in your absence.'

'But why should that 'someone' do that, I mean clean up and cook?'

'You have a point there, Varun said thoughtfully. Maybe he or she has a soft corner for you and wants you to be comfortable during your maid's absence?'

'That doesn't make sense', Mini said.

Varun thought for a while. 'I think I have got an idea.' He said excitedly.

Mini and Ria looked at him in questioning eyes.

'Why don't you install a CCTV camera in your house? That way you can capture the unknown intruder.'

'Sounds good,' Mini said, feeling a bit relieved.' I will do that. Thanks Varun. But listen to me both of you, do not say a word to anyone about this.'

That evening too, on her return Mini found all the lights switched on, her dinner ready in the microwave oven, her bed made and all the clothes neatly folded.

'I must get the CCTV camera installed tomorrow,' she decided before going to sleep.

But it took two more days to get the camera installed. It was only on the fifth day the camera was set and connected to her laptop. Varun and Ria enquired if she had installed the camera or not.

'Not yet,' Mini lied. She did not want to share her discovery, if at all there was something to discover, with neither of them nor with anyone else for that matter.

Mini returned in the evening to find her house in total darkness. It was a busy day for her. There were back-to-back calls from the clients, and she did not have a moment's free time. She was curious to know if the strange do-gooder had paid a visit to her apartment or not thast day. She unlocked the latch and went in. it was very dark inside. She switched on the light. The room looked shabby and unclean. She went to the kitchen. The plates and bowls were still in the sink, unwashed. She opened the door of the microwave oven. It was empty.

'Hmm! Clever indeed!' Mini smiled knowingly. 'The friendly ghost has somehow come to know about the camera and skipped its routine visit,'

She made an online order for a pizza, ate it while watching the television. 'There would be no more such unwanted visits,' she thought with relief and went to sleep. The dream too did not visit her sleep that night.

She slid out of the bed, feeling fresh and relaxed and walked out of the room. She stopped abruptly. The unseen visitor had returned, the house looked very clean. It has been swept and mopped. She saw that the toaster was switched on and steam spiralled out the glass of the milk. Mini waited to hear the sound of the front door closing. Nothing. There was complete silence in the house except the soft hum of the refrigerator. Driven by an uncanny curiosity she pulled open the door of the refrigerator. There were a couple of cartons of milk, a packet of bread and fresh fruits in it.

Mini recollected that she had decided last evening to buy bread and fruit while returning from the office. But she felt tired after the busy hours and had postponed the shopping to the next day. Then who had brought all these items?

Shivering a little inwardly Mini walked into the washroom. After taking bath she got into the formal outfit for the office and sat down to her breakfast. She was afraid that if she watched the footage in her house the person who made these clandestine visits would be warned. So, she was in a hurry to reach the office and see the recorded footage.

She drove fast to the office. 'You are early, madam,' the security guard greeted her with a genial smile.

'Yes,' she said shortly returning his smile and walked briskly to the elevator without giving him a scope to stretch the conversation. She took out the laptop and switched it on, clicked the playback button to enter the menu. Her fingers trembling, she selected the channel and the video type. Then she clicked the start button and waited, holding her breath.

The inside of her house flashed on the screen of the laptop. Everything was clearly visible. It was the footage of that morning. She shifted to the edge of the chair and watched in unblinking eyes.

Nothing happened for a minute or so, and then suddenly a figure came into sight. It was a woman wearing a floral print sari, her hair held in a knot at the back of her head. She was holding the broom and sweeping the floor of the living room. Then she went into the kitchen and put the milk to boil. She came out, put the breads in the toaster. She came into bedroom, changed the bedspread and the pillow covers. Her back was turned to the camera all the time she worked. The figure and the sari both looked closely familiar. But the real shock came when Mini discovered that the bed was empty. How could that be? She was supposed to be sleeping there. It was still not daylight and she remembered she had woken up after the sunrise as she did most days.

Then she remembered the floral print sari. It belonged to her mother, the sari which was one of the few Mini had cherished all these years. She waited, her heart hammering, blood racing hotly in her veins.

'Mother?' Her spirit?

The woman was walking to the front door. She turned as she opened the door and looked straight into the camera.

Mini let out a thin scream.

The face that stared at her from the screen was her own.

****

The Fortune Teller

The strident ringing of the land phone woke Myra up. There was a click followed by father's voice..

Hello!

In that state of half wakefulness Myra was not interested nor able to know the caller and the subject of the conversation.

'Where are you, Subhadra? Come here.'

Her father called out to her mother. There was something odd in his tone that brought Myra fully awake.

What is it?

Subhadra asked, sounding a little concerned as she walked into the living room.

'They are asking for a motorcar.'

Motor car?

Subhadra slumped down on the sofa and stared at her husband.

'But they said they would not want anything except the bare minimum we would gift our daughter depending on what our financial condition permits,' she said brokenly after some time.

Myra was now listening intently, her ears picking out every word.

'I know. This is just a pretext to reject the proposal. I had never expected these people to behave like the others did. They appeared so sensible and so down to earth!'

'What could we do except enduring the humiliation.' Subhadra breathed out a heavy sigh.

Myra's eyes burned with unshed tears.

This was the third time the family of the prospective groom had said no to the proposal taking one or other kind of an excuse. Myra was a plain looking girl, the run of the mill type. A round face with pair of not so big eyes, thick dark eyebrows that joined over the bridge of her nose that was neither sharp nor flat made her an average looking girl. She was short heighted and had a wheatish complexion. She knew that she was not beautiful in the accepted sense and that was the reason why the suitors were reluctant to go ahead with the proposal. It was extremely embarrassing and humiliating to sit silently before strangers holding her face down while three or four pairs of appraising eyes scanned her looks.

Myra was the second of the two daughters.

Her father who was a bank employee had retired from service a year back. Her elder sister was married off to a decent person who also was an employee in a bank. Myra worked as an assistant librarian in the City college. She was an amicable person and everyone in the college liked her for her friendly and unpretentious behaviour. She was sincere to her duty too. All put together Myra was happy with her life until this charade of the ' seeing the prospective bride' episodes started some seven to eight months back. Despite Myra's protests her father who was more than interested to fulfil his filial duty kept looking for a suitable candidate for his daughter. During the past six months two supposed -to -be grooms accompanied by friends and relatives had paid visits to Myra's house. Myra, acting upon the advice of her mother, had donned herself in an expensive sari, served them tea and snacks, and kept sitting before them like an item displayed in an exhibition waiting to be assessed. They would cast a look of appraisal over her, ask a few questions, assure her parents of an early reply from their side, and leave. A week or so later the mediating fellow would call to inform her parents that the groom's family was not interested in the proposal. After two such episodes Myra had sternly denied to make herself an object of humiliation. But her father had coaxed her to put up with the embarrassment for one last time with a promise that he would never ask her for a repeat performance. He was hopeful that everything would be fine until the phone rang that afternoon. Myra slid off the bed and walked into the living room. Her parents sat on the sofa, silent and glum.

'Never mind father,' she said trying to take the edge off their desperateness, 'I knew this was going to happen. I have told you several times that I am not too eager to marry now. But you will not listen to me. Why not wait and leave things to take their own course? I do not understand why you are so very inclined to throw me out of your house,' she said and smiled broadly to make it sound light. Her father touched her face affectionately.

'You have a point there. Let us wait patiently and let events take their own course. And do not ever say again that we are eager to send you out of this house,'

'I hope you would keep your promise, father. You would not make me stand before strangers like a made-up puppet anymore.'

'Alright dear. I will leave it in the hands of God from now on.' Her father said resignedly.

'Let us wait and hope that everything will be set right soon.' Mother said.

Myra breathed a sigh of relief.

Two uneventful months passed. Days and nights followed one another routinely. Myra went to college regularly and was happy that the mediating man had not brought any other proposal. Her parents seemed to have reconciled to the inevitable and waited patiently for things to turn corner.

That afternoon it rained heavily. A storm wind blew at a great speed. It kept Myra and her friend Kriti who worked as a junior librarian in the same college, detained in the college for a long time. After about an hour the rain stopped, and the wind slowed down. They came out to the road. But they could not find an empty autorickshaw to get back home. They had to travel in opposite directions, and they needed two rickshaws. But there was not a single rickshaw that did not carry passengers more than its capacity.

'Let us walk up to the next chowk and have some tea. There is no point in waiting here.'

'Fine. A hot cup of tea might give us an idea to solve the problem.'

So, they walked chatting, and looking at the shops on either side of the road.

'Hey, look at that.' Kriti said suddenly.

Myra's gaze followed her friend's. Squeezed between a small hotel and a beauty parlour there was a small door on which was written in letters of faded silver 'KNOW YOUR FUTURE.'

Should we go in? Kriti looked expectantly at her friend.

'What on earth for? I do not believe in these things. All these clairvoyance is pure trash.' Myra moved on

'But I do. Why not give me company? I want to know when they are promoting me to the post of Asst. Librarian and you can also ask about your marriage.'

'I am not interested.' Myra said shortly. But Kriti would not give up. Finally, she persuaded Myra, and both walked up to the door. It seemed closed. Myra looked for a bell but there was none. She gave a light push and the door opened. They walked in. A young boy wearing a uniform sat behind a rickety table on which there was a visitors' register. He looked up at them and asked their names. After entering the names in the register, he got to his feet.

'Please wait here. I will inform madam.' He said politely.

Myra and Kriti looked at each other.

'Madam? Seems quite posh.' Myra said with a smile that could have been a blend of surprise and sarcasm.

'You can go in now.' The boy said, returning.

They went inside.

The interior was in sharp contrast to the

modest, unassuming facade. The room was big, spacious, and brightly lit. On the panelled walls were old tapestries with strange scenes worked on them. Curtains of velvet and silk draped the windows. The room was furnished with taste and style. There was a massive, heavily cushioned settee that spelt money and luxury. An ornate bowl of silver containing a bunch of freshly cut roses stood on the big oval glass-topped table behind which sat a woman of about fifty flashing her diamond earrings at them. Her attractive face wore a welcoming smile.

'Please come in. Have a seat.'

Myra and Kriti greeted her back and sat down.

'Want to know your future?' She asked without waiting to make small talks.

'Yes', Kriti said promptly.

'Please come here.'

Kriti wandered to the oval table. 'Sit', the woman pointed to an artistically designed wooden stool by her side. Kriti took her place on the stool and waited. A delicate looking thumb flashing a diamond finger-ring pressed a bell under the edge of the table. A maid like character appeared instantly as if she was ready for it carrying a coffee mug. She put it before Kriti.

'Drink it.' Madam said.

Kriti turned to look at Myra who watched her uneasily.

'Drink it. Nothing will happen ...' Madam assured Kriti drank the coffee in a few large swallows.

The coffee was only slightly warm. The sediments looked a blackish brown at the bottom of the cup. Madam took the cup from her hand and peered into it.

'You have a job issue.'

'Why yes! How did you...'

Never mind that. You will have to wait for the brush flowers to bloom.'

'Brush flowers? In what way the brush flower is linked to my promotion?' Kriti asked, bewildered.

'Wait for the brush flowers to bloom,' Madam repeated and flicked her fingers in a gesture of dismissal. Kriti , looking flustered, returned to the settee.

Madam motioned Myra to come and take her place on the stool beside her. There was an action replay. The maid brought in the black lukewarm coffee and Myra drank it. The coffee tasted strong and bitter. Madam peered at the sediments while Myra watched her anxiously. After a minute which seemed to be a perpetuity to Myra Madam turned her big, penetrating eyes to Myra.

'Do not worry.' She said with a smile. 'Your prince charming will come riding a horse!'

Now it was Myra's turn to look bewildered.

She had not said even a word about her bungled up marriage proposals to this woman and here she has come up with a reading!! But she did not say anything and rose to her feet.

'Four hundred' Madam said.

Without a word Myra unzipped her handbag, took out a couple of two hundred rupees notes and put them on the table. The madam repeated her finger flicking act, gesturing them to leave.

Out in the thin darkness of the approaching evening, Kriti looked at Myra, an uneasy smile hovering on her lips.

'What a waste of hard-earned money!! I am sorry. ' Kriti said apologetically.

'Forget it,' Myra said. ' I had warned you. These fortune tellers are a bunch of cheat'.

An autorickshaw pulled up on the roadside. The driver looked expectantly at them.

We would need two. Kriti said.

Another one cruised in even as Kriti spoke. They got into the rickshaws and headed towards their homes that were in different directions.

Father did not ask Myra again to appear before the strange visitors of the supposed to- be- groom's family. But as days passed, he looked more and more worried. Myra could do nothing about it except blaming her own destiny.

'Have you bought the gift for Shovan sir?' Kriti asked.

'Not yet. I will buy it this afternoon while returning home. '

'Let us visit that new gift shop downtown. They say that one can find many varieties of traditional as well as modern gift items there.'

'Fine. We will try the one.'

'We will leave here a little early or else we will be late for the party. We will have to go home first.

'Yes. Let us start at 3 pm. We will have sufficient time in our hands for getting ready for the party if we make it that early.

Myra consented.

A newly married young professor in the college was hosting a party. Most of the staff could not attend the marriage function because they had to travel to his village which was in a different state. So, he organized a special wedding reception exclusively for the college staff.

Myra gave a gentle push to the polished glass door and entered. Kriti followed. The interior of the shop was brilliantly lit from the several tiny, almost invisible light bulbs fitted in the chandeliers that hung from the ceiling. It flaunted glass panelled show cases on either side of the aisle. There was a small crowd, and the salesmen and women were busy displaying attractive artifacts before the prospective buyers. A young boy noticed Myra and Kriti and approached them.

'Yes ma'am. Can I help you?'

Myra's gaze wandered over the figurines, statues and framed pictures in a comparatively larger glass case. Kriti looked at the ornate flower vases and fancy handbags.

Could you show that brass flower vase, please,' Kriti said

'Sure ma'am. The young boy took out the vase and put it on the display table.

'You can see the others too ma'am, the young boy said, giving her that artificial smile the salesmen keep reserved for the customers. He brought out a few more items and placed it in front of her.

Kirti pointed at a white and black sophisticated looking ladies' handbag.

'Show me that handbag, please' Kriti asked thinking that a handbag may be an appropriate gift for Shovan Sir's wife.

'Sure, ma'am,'

The over-eager young boy took it out for Kriti's inspection.

All the time Kriti was busy selecting her gift, Myra looked at the statues and paintings. There were acrylic paintings and oil paintings. Myra could not make up her mind and stood undecided looking helplessly at the glass case.

'Can I help you?'

A voice spoke behind her.

She turned abruptly and almost collided with the man.

'Excuse me' Myra said, 'Do I know you?'

'Of course not. I happen to be a friend of the owner's son. He is not here now, and I am in charge, if you could call it that.'

He flashed a disarming smile at her.

'I was watching you. You seem to be interested in the paintings. So I thought if I could help you in making a choice..'

'Thank you. Actually, I am not sure which one of these I should go for.'

'I will try to select something if you permit me.'

'Please'

The man who introduced himself as the friend of the owner's son took out a few paintings.

He spread them out on the display table. A beautiful autumn landscape, a woman silhouetted against a silver moon, a mosaic Buddha , a sea scape , a peacock and a peahen ......bound in black and brown and silver and gold lined frames.

Myra fingered the paintings and looked undecidedly at the show case.

'Here. Take a look at this.'

The young man picked out another that stood partially hidden behind the picture of a ferry in a moonlit river.

Myra flicked a glance at the painting the man held out. It was a silver framed painting of a pair of horses, one a little ahead of the other, galloping on. The snow-white horses were in sharp contrast with the dark backdrop they were painted against and looked very alive as if they would leap out of the frame at that very moment and gallop away. Myra looked at the painting with interest.

'Yes,' she thought, 'this is a good one. There is no point in wasting more time here.'

'Please gift wrap it.' She said aloud.

'Sure,' the man handed the painting to a boy for getting it gift wrapped. By that time Kriti too had chosen her gift. After much deliberation she had finally settled for a fancy flower vase of bell metal. They both stood waiting at the counter while the girl did the billing. The man came back.

'Will you please give us your address and phone number so that we can inform you when there is a discount sale or any such good offer.' He said politely. Kriti gave her address.

Myra hesitated. 'I do not share my number with strangers, she said. I can give my home address only.'

'No issues. Home address will do.'

The man wrote down the address of both Myra and Kriti. The salesboy put the neatly packed gift items in two carry bags and handed one to each.

It was about two months after the party at the professor's house. Myra was busy in cataloguing the books which were to be transferred to the seminar library of different departments. She was a bit rushed because she had to complete the cataloguing before the puja holidays that was to start after two days.

Kriti scuttled in, her face flushing in excitement.

'What happened?' Myra inquired. 'Why are you so excited?'

'Guess what?'

'No suspense. ... come out with your secret.' Myra laughed.

Kriti dangled a brown envelope in front of her.

'What is it?'

'See it for yourself.'

Myra took out the letter from the envelope and let her eyes run over the contents.

Kriti was promoted to the post of Asst. Librarian.

'My God! What a marvellous piece of news,' she embraced Kriti. ' Congratulations, dear. I am so happy for you.'

Tears of joy swam in Kriti's eyes.

The other staff members came to the library and congratulated Kriti.

'This calls for a party,' one of them said.

Yes , we want a party Kriti madam. Others said in a chorus.

Myra and Kriti went to an ice cream parlour for a mini celebration. Kriti was very happy and Myra was happy for her friend.

The sun has set by the time they got out of the parlour. The cloudless early autumn sky was wrapped in grey. They got into two autorickshaws and headed home.

Myra's mother stood at the front gate waiting for her daughter. Myra felt a bit guilty. She had not even called home to inform that she would be late.

'I am so sorry mama,' she apologised. 'It so happened that Kriti got the orders of her promotion today. So, both of us went to have some ice cream and got delayed.

'No problem, dear, her mother said fondly. I just could not wait to tell you the news.' Myra's curious gaze travelled to her mother's face. Her lips were curled in a strange smile.

'What is it, mama? Why do you look do mysterious?' Myra asked, feeling a bit confused.

'Come inside and get freshened up first.'

Her mother said and turning walked into the house.

Wondering vaguely what the cause of her happiness could possibly be, Myra followed her.

Father was sitting on a rocking chair on the front veranda speaking to someone on his mobile phone. Myra walked past him her ears involuntarily capturing snatches of the conversation.

'We have no objection. We just want to keep the ring-exchange event a simple affair since the formal engagement ceremony will be performed within a month. ..

His voice faded as she moved further inside and entered her room. She went into the washroom and changed into a pair of cotton salwar and kurta.

Her mother had dished out hot pancakes made of rice and black gram paste and a big dollop of spicy chutney to go with it. Myra sat down to eat. Mother lowered herself into another chair beside her.

'Will you please cut the suspense now, mana, ' Myra said. ' It seems to me a day of surprises for me. First Kriti and then you...'

'The boy's parents had come here in the afternoon. They are very much interested in the proposal. Their son does not even want to see you, they say. But they want the marriage to be solemnized at the earliest. '

'Marriage? Whose marriage?'

'Yours, obviously. Who else?'

'How could you decide everything without even asking me for once?' Myra sounded hurt.

'We have not committed anything. How could we do that without your consent? But they seem to be good people, simple and straight. They boy is their only child. He works as an electrical engineer in the Indian Railways,

They have brought a photograph of him. Decide after you look at it. Ultimately it is your decision, dear. We can always say no.'

Myra was both shocked and surprised at the sudden turn of events. Who would want to marry a girl without seeing her, she wondered. Even the parents did not want to see the girl they were to take as a bride into their family. It was hard to believe.

'It seems the boy has seen you somewhere before. The truth is that they had called a few days ago. I did not tell you about it because I and your father did not expect it to materialize so soon.' Myra's mother added.

'Seen me? Where? Myra wondered and tried to recollect the recent happenings. She could remember nothing significant.

'Here, take a look'. Mother handed the passport size photo to Myra. Myra cast a brief glance at it not showing much interest. The face of a young man with a mass of black hair, kind eyes under thick brows, a well-shaped nose and a smiling mouth gazed back at her. The face looked familiar in a way. Where had she seen him? Then she remembered and her heart began to beat faster. It was the young man in the gift shop. The man who had chosen the painting of the horses for her!!

Horses!!

The words of a strange looking woman wearing shining earrings of diamond flashed before her with the speed of lightning.

'Your prince charming will come riding a horse....!!!'

She was right after all..

'Oh My God!' The words spurted out of her mouth before she realized.

'What is it, dear?' Myra's mother asked anxiously. 'We can always say no if you do not agree to the proposal...'

'It is nothing mother,' Myra said. ' I just remembered I had seen him in a shop' ..

'Do you want us to go ahead with it?' Mother looked expectantly at Myra.

'If you and father think it is okay, I have no objection,' Myra said, blushing.

Her mother took Myra in her arms and kissed her forehead. Tears glistened in her eyes.

A few days after the date of marriage was fixed in a formal ring ceremony.

'Did they like the painting which I had chosen?' her would-be -groom asked, an amused twinkle in his eyes.

Myra smiled shyly.

'Yes! The horses changed everything!'

An overjoyed Kriti hugged Myra tightly. ' I am so, so happy' ..

Do you remember the fortune teller Madam, Kriti?

Myra asked as they were returning to Myra's house after the ceremony was over.

'Of course, I remember her. She had swindled four hundred rupees out of us.'

'She hadn't. She was right in her predictions.'

'How could you say that?'

'Didn't she say that my groom will come riding a horse? It sounded so absurd at that time. But it was that painting of the horse which in its own mysterious way has brought us together.'

Kriti gaped at Myra as the truth of what she said began to sink in.

'You are right!' She said in excitement. 'It has proved true in your case. What about me?'

'She was also right when she said that your job issues would be solved when the brush flowers bloomed. Didn't you get your promotion letter in the early autumn, just before the puja holidays, when the brush flowers began blooming by the riversides?'

'Oh yes, *yes!!*'

Kriti' eyes opened wide.

'So, the Madam was not a cheat, ' she exclaimed. 'We just failed to gather the meaning.'

'Why don't we go and meet her? Just a formal visit, to say our thanks?'

'That's a good idea. We shall go and meet her tomorrow.'

The afternoon was ripe when the friends reached the place. A construction work was going on. Men were at work digging the sides of the road. A couple of JCB machines almost blocked the path. Myra looked around but could not locate the modest door that held the sign ' KNOW YOUR FUTURE' in faded silver.

In fact, all the roadside shops were demolished by the Municipality for the execution of a road widening scheme. Myra and Kriti returned with heavy hearts.

' Did the Madam know she would have to leave here for good? Let her be happy wherever she is, and let her make the right predictions to people in her weird ways,'

Myra wished silently as the autorickshaw threaded its way noisily through the streaming traffic.

******

The Live Painting

Ours was an arranged marriage. Kabir and I did not see much of each other before the engagement ceremony. After our engagement we chatted over phone when both of us were free. When the marriage proposal came up father told me about it and sought my opinion. He was, as far as the views of my parents and senior members of my family were concerned, an ideal choice. He was his parents' only child. His father and mother both had retired from their government jobs. Though they were natives of Odisha, they had settled in Mumbai and lived in a posh house of their own in Malad. Kabir was posted as a senior associate in a research laboratory on a lucrative pay scale. We had met for the first time on the day Kabir and his parents made a formal visit to our house. The gentleman who was mediating the proposal too had accompanied them. After my successful performance of the ritualistic charade of serving tea and refreshments our parents suggested us to have a person-to-person interaction for a better understanding of each other and conveniently went out of the room to sit in the enclosed but spacious balcony.

Left to ourselves we just sat looking down at the floor, each of us filled with curiosity and questions.

Kabir was the first, as it was obvious in the given situation, to break the silence.

'What do you like to do as a pastime? I understand you are a student of humanities. You must be interested in art and literature, aren't you?'

'Yes, I love to read. Mostly I read novels and poems. I have a passion for music and painting though I can neither paint nor sing.' I replied.

Kabir smiled. 'I wonder how we are going to put up with each other. You know I do not understand much of aesthetics. But I have a great regard for music and panting.'

I could realize that Kabir was a level- headed and down to earth gentleman who was passionate about his research. The next two things he was interested in was sports and politics.

Romanticism was not his cup of tea. I was just the opposite. I had an aesthetic temperament. The changing contours of nature as the seasons come and go filled me with romantic thoughts. Rains inspired poetry in me the same way as the autumn sky and the dropping leaves did.

I was feeling a bit sceptical about my future with a realistic man like Kabir. But my parents liked him a lot, and I did not have the heart to disappoint by rejecting the alliance just because Kabir did not have a romantic strain in his character. But I had read somewhere that if both the spouses shared the same temperament the married life might not be too easy. Too much of romanticism or too much of pragmatism might upset the balance in one's married life. On the other hand if the partners are of different mindsets it helps to keep the equilibrium undisturbed. During my brief and infrequent meetings with Kabir before our marriage I had learnt that he was a warm, kind-hearted gentleman with engaging manners. He could get reasonably emotional despite his matter-of-fact approach to life. I hoped that our marriage would not be as difficult as I presumed it to be and decided to resign to the inevitable.

The marriage was solemnized with the routine pomp and splendour as it happens in most cases.

I came to live with Kabir and his parents in his house at Mumbai.

Finally, the hangover of the ceremony lifted and the rush and the excitement settled down. Kabir and I decided to take a look at the gifts we received. We put the gift packets on the floor and sorted them according to their sizes. First, we unwrapped the relatively smaller packets. There were expensive as well as ordinary gifts. Most of them, when opened, revealed figurines, books, perfume and things like that. The bigger ones contained kitchen wares, makeup kits, saris and dresses, and other such items. Kabir had a comment ready for each of the gifts and its giver. I was amazed at his sense of humour. He was a person one can easily and effortlessly get along with. He seemed to have a knack to entertain people around him with his light-hearted talks. After the small and relatively bigger packets were opened, we tried the ones which looked larger in size but thinner in volume. Must be paintings and wall hangings,' Kabir speculated. He was right. As we tore open the wraps of the packets one after another beautiful paintings and wall hanging spilled out of it. All those revealed the aesthetic sense of the people who selected them. We had opened all the packets except the last one. Kabir cut open the packet and pulled out the thing inside.

'Wow!' I caught my breath sharply as Kabir held it before me. It was something divine! A painting of the moon over the surface of a wavy sea. The sky and the sea were painted in almost similar shades, an artistic blend of dark blue and grey. The curves of the of the sea were touched with an off-white shade to create the impression of the foamy tides. The amber moon was so close to the surface of the sea that it looked as if it was floating over the water. There was a lone white boat that seemed to be sailing towards the sky, slightly slanting up as if to touch the moon. It was simply mesmerizing!!

'How enchanting a boat ride in such a night must be!! The sea spraying the mist on your face, the moon bending down to reach the water and the enigmatic blue silence all around!!' I blurted out involuntarily forgetting that Kabir was watching me intently, amused and amazed.

I stopped short, feeling embarrassed to have exposed the romantic contour of my character unabashedly in front of a man whom I knew for just a fortnight or so.

Kabir smiled understandingly.

'It is alright. There is nothing wrong in getting carried away by its beauty. This painting is really something exceptional. The sea and the moon look so captivating. But the sea always looks lovely when viewed from far. I don't think it is as much mesmerizing at a close view from the boat, especially in the night! Things that appear enchanting from a distance do not always look the same when viewed from close quarters.'

I did not say anything. I knew Kabir would not take it the way I did. Silently I collected the discarded wrappers and went out of the room.

A surprise awaited me sometime later. When I came to our bedroom after dinner, I saw the painting hanging on the wall. The wall, painted in glossy white, offered a splendid contrast to the blue -black sea and the night sky.

'Looks really enchanting' isn't it?'

Kabir smiled and put his arms around me. I felt happy. At least he was not as dry of feelings as I thought him to be!

Living in Kabir's family I have experienced the joy of fulfilment. Kabir's parents were so caring that I, not even for once, felt that I am away from my own father and mother.

+++++

I sat looking out of the window at the gathering clouds in the sky. Kabir was out at his laboratory. His parents were downstairs watching TV. It began to rain soon. The trees drooped under the driving sheet of rain. There were occasional lightnings followed by the rumbles of thunder. I always loved to watch the rain. I used to come out and get wet in the rain ignoring my mother's admonition. Once when I was returning from school it began to rain hard. I and my friend walked down holding an umbrella over our head. Suddenly a blast of wind blew the umbrella away and flung it into the rushing water on the street. We ran after the umbrella, splashing our feet in the rainwater, giggling in excitement. My lips curled up involuntarily in a smile as I recalled the incident.

I looked down wistfully at the young and middle-aged couples in raincoats and mackintoshes riding bikes in the rain and felt a bit disappointed. How I would have loved to go on a long bike ride with Kabir in the rain!! I had once said that to him, too. His eyes twinkled in amusement might be because he thought the idea to be an absurd one. 'The rainy way to catch cold!' He said and smiled. Being a man with a scientific bent of mind Kabir could think of only the impact rain on the physical condition. It would be a vain effort to make him realize how rain affects the heart.

I came out of the room and climbed up the steps leading to the roof, unlatched the door that opened to the terrace and went into the rain. I stood there closing my eyes, feeling the dull, warm trains of water soaking my body. Were Kabir there with me!! Several scenes from the romantic movies I had watched flashed past my mind making my heart throb with ecstasy and I trembled a little. Later when the rain finally stopped, I came back and changed into dry clothes.

That night I told Kabir about my adventure in the terrace, hoping he would regret his absence there. But his reaction was totally different. 'Why on earth did you have to do that?' He sat up , looking concerned. 'It is so childish. You may fall sick. Take some anti-allergen before going to sleep,' he advised. I felt a sharp prick at my heart. Was it a mistake to marry a person like Kabir? I strongly believed that the newly wed couples must indulge in such romantic gestures now and then. But Kabir would not understand. He would never be impressed by the fragrance of the spring, the warmth of the slanting rains, or the enigma of the moonlit sea!!

' Sorry, ' I said gloomily, 'I shouldn't have done that or at least I wouldn't have told you about it.'

Kabir looked at me closely for a while. There was a mysterious look in his eyes. He slid off the bed, rummaged in the medicine drawer and took out an anti-allergen tablet. He poured water into a glass and came back.

'Here, take it.' He held out the tablet and glass of water. Without saying a word, I swallowed the tablet. I tuned on my side. The painting of the moonlit sea hung on the wall that faced me. I looked for a long time at it and then closed my eyes.

+++

The change was too small to be noticed, but I could sense it in Kabir's behaviour. He had become more caring and sensitive. Whenever he bought books and science journals for himself, he never forgot to bring a title from Sarah MacLean or Carolyn Brown for me. One day he surprised me by bringing a *gajra* (a flower garland for a lady's hair) of jasmines. I felt a bit uneasy. Was he trying to go out of his way to please me? No one should go against one's nature to please another, be the one is a husband or a wife!! But I could not say anything to Kabir. He, however, was always his jovial self while interacting with me. May be, I had behaved in a childish way by getting drenched in the rain. I felt a tingle of embarrassment.

The months of rain departed making way for a calm, solemn autumn. I always loved the cloudless autumn sky, the slow yellowing of the leaves and the clumps of cottonwool like kans-grass swaying beside the rivers and lakes. I missed the autumn of my hometown. But as it happened always, I felt my spirit soothed by an autumnal calm. Life was moving on smoothly with Kabir. Both of us had got over the differences in our temperaments and enjoyed the bliss of togetherness.

Kabir came back early that day. It was not even five in the afternoon. I and my parents- in-law had just finished our tea. Kabir's mother was preparing for the evening worship.

'Get ready. We are going out.' Kabir announced coming into the kitchen. I kept the washed cups in the cabinet carefully and glanced at him, mildly surprised.

'Where?' I asked.

'You just get ready. No more questions.' He smiled.

I sought permission from my mother- in -law who readily agreed.

'Where are you taking me?' I asked again as Kabir made the car worm through the late afternoon traffic.

'Do not be so impatient. Just wait and watch!' He replied, his gaze fixed on the road. We stopped at the Gateway of India. The place was teeming with tourists and street vendors. I glanced around at the heterogeneous crowd while Kabir looked for a convenient parking spot. Finally, he found one and after parking the car returned to the place where I stood.

He caught hold of my hand and guided me through the swarms of people towards the jetty. I struggled along the narrow bumpy slope down to the edge of the water where several large and small motor-run ferries as well as rowboats were docked. A middle-aged man who was sitting at the wheel of a glossy two seater motorboat stood up and saluted Kabir.

'Ready?' Kabir asked him.

'All set Sa'ab,' the man showed a row of decayed, yellowish teeth in a genial grin.

'Let's start then', Kabir said.

'Sure Sa'ab. As soon as you and Mem Saab climb down here ...'

Kabir and I walked down the rickety looking gangplank and stepped into the boat. I looked at him, wondering why so unexpectedly he had made this programme. He was watching me.

'Don't look so puzzled. I had long since planned a boat ride with you in a moonlit night. But I was getting caught up in various kinds works. I am free this evening. And so, I decided to take you on boat ride in the sea, and note the coincidence dear, it is a full moon night. I think you have a long-cherished wish to boat in a moonlit sea. Don't you?'

I did not say anything to that. I was glad that Kabir respected my feelings, but there was a tinge somewhere in the heart that he was trying to adopt himself to my moods. At that moment I loved him more than I ever did. 'Thank you. I had not expected that my wish will be fulfilled in this way,'

Kabir's hand closed on mine. The ferryman started the engine and the boat slithered into the open sea. The glowing lights at the Gateway of India began to recede to the background as we moved forward. Soon they were not seen any longer. It was a full moon night and the tides rose higher than they did in ordinary days. Wrapped in the wispy dark of the evening the boat glided on, its bow cleaving apart the foamy water. The wind felt slightly cold. I trembled a little. Kabir took off his coat and put it on my shoulders. I nudged closer to him, and he twined his arm around me. 'Look up there,' he pointed at the sky. A big moon that looked like a silver platter was coming out of the sea. I stared at it, entranced.

We had left the land far behind. The sea was all around us, spread out unendingly. The waves began to rise higher and higher. It seemed we were the only three living beings trapped between the sea and the sky. I felt a frisson of fear. My grip around Kabir's hand tightened a bit. Kabir looked at me. 'It's beautiful, isn't it?' He asked. I nodded, not feeling so sure. The sea was now roaring loudly. The undulating waves ahead and around looked like hills of black liquid. The moon now had climbed up and was floating just over our heads.

Suddenly the engine of the boat gave out a spurt and died. The boat stopped.

'What happened Binayak?' Kabir asked.

' Some problem in the engine, Sa'ab, I will fix it soon. You do not worry.'

'A lone boat in the mid sea, under a magical full moon .... exactly like that painting. Isn't it?' Kabir looked at me closely, a small smile hovering on his face.

I looked up at the sky without saying a word. The moon that hung precariously over the boat looked as if it would drop any moment on it.

I wanted to go back...to the safety of the land, back to our cosy house. The sea and the moon had lost all their charm, and the romantic strain in me had given way to alarm. 'What if the engine did not start? What if we are stranded here, in the midst of these swelling waves? What if the boat got capsized..?' So many 'ifs'. I could not think beyond it. I was feeling numb. I closed my eyes tightly and began to say silent prayers. 'Please God! Save us. What a fool I was to wish to enjoy a boat ride in a moonlit sea! I will never ever wish for any such thing.' I promised to God and to myself. I had no idea when tears of helplessness had begun to roll down my eyes until I felt Kabir's hand on my face. He wiped my tears. 'There is nothing to panic. The engine will be fixed soon. Let us enjoy this magic of the sea. It is as if the painting has come alive!'

'I do not want to enjoy. I want to go back home. ' I said, my voice hoarse in fear.

'Oh God, please save us!' I said aloud. As if an answer to my prayer the engine let out a loud sputtering sound.

'It is okay Sa'ab. The engine is alright now. Would you like to go a little farther?'

'No.' I broke in loudly before Kabir could say anything. 'Let's go back.'

'Yes. Let's go back,' Kabir said.

'As you wish, Sa'ab', Binayak said and turned the boat. Kabir and I did not speak a word to each other during the ride back. It was past nine when we reached the jetty. The Gateway of India was still heavily crowded. I got down. As I waited for Kabir to come after making the payment to Binayak, I silently offered my gratitude to God Almighty for saving us. We drove back home in silence.

Dinner over I came to our bedroom. Kabir was leafing through a science magazine propped up on a pillow. He looked up at me as I entered.

'Tired?' He asked.

'Exhausted, ' I agreed.

'Go to sleep. You will feel better in the morning. I will just finish this piece and go to sleep too.'

I lay down on my side. The painting of the boat in the moonlit sea faced me. I closed my eyes. I recollected the bizarre happenings of the evening. Suddenly a thought struck me like a bolt of lightning.

Why did the boat stop in the mid-sea so abruptly? Was it incidental or pre-planned? Had Kabir and the boatman Binayak worked in cahoots to frighten me? No, no! Kabir could not do that to me. I needed one such experience to come out of my world of romantic fantasy. I opened my eyes and glanced at the painting. It seemed to have lost its magic!

'The first thing I will do tomorrow after Kabir leaves for his laboratory is, take the painting off the bedroom wall and put it somewhere else, out of sight!' I promised to myself and shut my eyes.

*****

Angel's Anklet

It was still a bit dark. The skyline in the west was slowly getting clear. I opened the front door noiselessly, careful not to wake up my parents and came out. Closing the door softly behind me I jogged across the narrow street to reach the big park on the other side. I have a habit of getting up early in the morning and go for a half an hour jogging either on the road or a park. I am not a person who is absurdly health conscious like many young people of our time. But I am very particular about this early morning exercise. I enjoy walking and jogging in the cool morning air, breathing the calmness around me that gets occasionally disturbed by the sleepy warble of exotic birds and the murmur of the breeze-blown leaves in the trees around. Now and then the distant blares of automobiles cause irritating distraction, though. I have developed this habit since my college days and still practice it with an austerity.

After completing my post-graduation in Statistics from a recognized university I had joined the LIC services and got a posting at Latur, Maharastra. In the initial days I used to stay as a paying guest in the house of an amicable Maharastrian family. Later I shifted to a house in an apartment building located close to my office. My father, who has retired from service a year before, and my mother came to live with me. My mother is a sociable person and soon she got friendly with quite a number of families, despite her inability to communicate with the local language. She could manage to maintain a wholesome relationship with our neighbours using her broken Hindi. We had hired a couple of women to do the house cleaning and cooking. Father, too, had made quite an impression in the senior citizens' circle of the housing society and had a good number of friends. In short, we were living a happy and complacent life even though we were far away from our hometown.

Kusum auntie was mother's closest amongst all. Hers was not a Marathi but a Sindhi family. She was an expert cook and often brought us delicious Sindhi cuisines like stuffed parathas and okra curry which they called Bhindi Bhasar , sweetmeats of different varieties which she cooked herself. They were living at a different area earlier but now had shifted to this building. She had a son who lived in Dubai and a mentally retarded daughter who needed constant attention. Kusum auntie took extremely good care of her, but she was worried who would look after the girl when uncle and auntie won't be physically capable enough to do that. Despite her worries Kusum auntie always wore a smiling face. She was very talkative and kept engaged her listeners with her lively narration about the people around. Her tales were interspersed with interesting anecdotes that greatly entertained her audience. Her tales were mostly woven around the 1993 earthquake that had wreaked havoc on Latur and shattered the lives of the people with a vengeful violence.

'This place was not like the way you see it now,' she told. 'There was a big pool here at this spot where this building is constructed. The street is also constructed after that and the park, too. The land where the park is, was a residential area before the quake struck. Many well-to-do families lived in their own houses and bungalows there. The earthquake razed the structures and hit the families with the force of a huge runaway train. Many of the people who lived there succumbed to the calamity. I have heard that the rescue teams found a number of people, mostly women and children, buried under the rubbles. The earthquake happened at around four in the morning. Most people were in the bed, asleep. They could not find time to escape and died in their sleep. Those who survived had left the place for good and settled elsewhere.

The horrifying tales of the disaster narrated by Kusum auntie with meticulous details gave me the shivers. Looking at the elegantly structured buildings, malls, market places, parks and tree lined streets now, it was difficult to imagine the monstrous mayhem that had devastated the place nearly three decades ago.

I had completed the jogging exercise. I sat down on a bench and mopped my face and hands. The park and the street and the adjacent buildings looked fresh, now washed with soft light of the dawn. The park was getting crowded. People of different ages were beginning to stream into the park for the morning walk, yoga and other exercises. I do not like to exercise in a park crowded with people and that is the reason why I do not go into the insides of the park for my exercise. For the same reason I choose the pre-dawn hour for my jogging when it is less peopled. At that hour there will be only one or two walkers in the park and I am always done with my exercise before it is morning.

A cool breeze was blowing. September is always

a humid month in India, but the mornings are cool. Sometimes it rains in the afternoons and night and that keeps the grass wet. But there was no rain in the previous day and the ground was dry. I waited for a while to restore a normal breathing and then got up. I stepped on to the track and walked a little faster than my usual pace. I was to reach the office early that morning since a senior officer was making a visit to our branch office and we were to be present there before eight-thirty. As I was hurrying back home my eyes fell on a swing to my right, few meters away from the entrance. A small girl in a pink frock was sitting on it quietly. She turned to look at me as if she could guess I too was looking at her. In the faint light of the early morning her tiny face framed by a mass of dark hair glowed like an angel's. 'Who must be this girl,' I wondered, 'sitting alone here. Perhaps she had come with some elder member of her family, father or grandfather who was taking a walk or doing yoga.'

I did not have time to think more about that. I hastened back home, ate my breakfast and rode to the office. The girl on the swing went out of my mind soon.

The next couple of days passed uneventfully. They followed the regular pattern beginning with the jogging in the park, going to the office after breakfast, watching television for some time in the evening, talking to my parents and then to the bed.

I saw her again on Saturday. I sat on a park bench after the jogging, resting my body. She was sitting on another bench a little away from mine. She sat calmly. She must be coming here frequently with some elders of her family. I was coming to the park since a month or so, soon after shifting to this apartment building. I wondered how

I had missed her all these days. It was a big park. Perhaps she was sitting somewhere a bit inside of the park.

I turned my gaze towards her. As if she could sense it instinctively, she too turned her face to look at me. I gave her a smile. She did not smile back but got down from the bench and walked into the inside of the park. Driven by curiosity I followed her noiselessly, maintaining a safe distance, careful not to arouse suspicion in her mind. She walked to a spot where people were busy doing their regular workouts. I her saw move to a spot by the row of flowering bushes. A few kids were playing there.

'Hey, Rajesh!' Someone called from behind. I turned to look back. A young man of around twenty or twenty-two was waving at another youth who was running along the edges of the park. I looked back at the spot where the girl was standing. She had disappeared. I could have caught sight of her parents or the people she came with, had I not been distracted by the young man's voice. I would try another day, I decided and returned home.

Next week it rained most of the days. The jogging path had become squishy. The park remained comparatively less crowded during most part of the week. I went out to jog in my regular time. I looked at the swing and the bench, half hoping to see the little girl. I knew that no parents would allow their child to come out to the open in the wet weather. I did not know why, or how I had developed a liking for that kid, though she was a total stranger to me. More days passed. The girl did not return. Was she sick? I felt concerned somehow. The weather was nasty in the previous week. Maybe she has caught a cold or something, I tried to think logically. My office work kept me preoccupied and the picture of the girl was beginning to dim in my mind. Now and then while taking rest on the park bench after the jogging my expectant eyes were drawn towards the empty benches nearby. I watched the young parents entering the park, wondering if one of the pairs was accompanying the girl.

I saw her again, after more than a month.

It was mid-October and the nights were becoming longer. I waited for the dawn to break before I went out to jog. It was Dussera time and the atmosphere was festive. I was enjoying a week-long puja vacation because the office was shut for the festival. I jogged for a little longer than I usually did and sat on the park enjoying the morning breeze till it was fully lit up with the beams of the nascent sun.

I sensed her presence before I could see her. My gaze travelled in the direction of the bench to my right automatically. She sat their quietly as she always did, looking at the entrance of the park where joggers and walkers were entering in ones and twos. Careful not to arouse her suspicion I wandered leisurely over to the bench where she sat. She was alerted by the sound of the footsteps and turned towards me. I moved closer. 'Hello, there!', I smiled at her. She did not smile back in reply to encourage me. But I had decided not to give up.

'Have you come alone or with your parents?

She looked back into the depth of the park. I guessed that her father or mother or the person who had accompanied her might be somewhere inside the park. Since it was a big park, one cannot see its insides from the spot we were.

'Is your companion here?'

Without answering she pointed a tiny index finger towards the inside of the park.

'Where do you live?'

Once again, she pointed a finger towards the west side wall of the park. 'Over there.'

I let my eyes wander in the direction. But there was no residential area in the west side of the park. There was a big departmental store and a garment shop.

'By the way, what is your name?'

'Anjli.'

'That's a nice one. Syncs with 'angel'. And in which class you are? You must be a good student, aren't you?' I said encouragingly.

She did not reply to that. She appeared to be quite a laconic child.

'You didn't tell me which class you are in,' I said flashing a warm smile hoping it would thaw the cool indifference and hesitance of the strangerhood.

'Two,' she said looking down at the ground.

'And where is your school?' I asked, ready to carry on the conversation even though her answers were short and evasive. 'Won't you tell me the name of your school?' I prodded on.

She turned her face towards me before answering. A shadow of gloom hung over her face, and her eyes looked dull as if she were in some kind of pain. It made me a bit uneasy. Children of that age usually are playful and bubbling with energy. But not this one. I wondered what could have been the reason.

'Over there. Saint Convent school.' She said pointing her finger to the west side wall of the park. I smiled, amused at the way she pronounced it. 'The school must be named after some religious figure as Convent schools usually are, which she was not able to say correctly,' I thought and let it stop at that.

She rose to her feet and walked away into the interior of the park before I could ask anything else. I did not follow her this time. 'I will wait till she opens up to me,' I decided and walked back home.

She did not come the next day, nor the day after.

It was a Sunday. I was relaxing at home. Kusum auntie came with her special delicacies. She brought us koki, a thick and delicious paratha made by wheat flour, onion, pomegranate seeds, curry and coriander leaves cooked in desi ghee, and Vaishnu Bhaji, a special mixed-veg dish that was an in-between of a fry and a curry.

'Mmm! Smells so good!' I exclaimed as I sat beside her on the settee.

'How is the office work going, beta? She asked fondly.

'Fine, auntie.'

'And your work out? Are you going for your walk and exercise regularly?'

'She will not skip that,' mother cut in before I could answer. 'Come rain, come sunshine, nothing can stop her.'

'That is a very good habit. You must keep it up.'

We sat chitchatting on random subjects. Suddenly I remembered about the school the little girl had mentioned.

'Is there a school, a convent school for small children, off the west side of the park, Kusum auntie?

'A convent school? No, I don't think so. There is a Government Higher Secondary school at the chowk area. Why do you ask?' She looked at me questioningly.

'Just like that. I met a little girl in the park a few days ago. She told me that she studied in some Saint Convent school located somewhere to the west of the park.

'Wait, I remember now. There was a convent school close to the colony which was destroyed in the quake. Didn't I tell you that day that they have built the park there now? Your little friend in the park must be confused about the location of her school.' She smiled.

'Seems so,' I said and let it drop at that.

She did not come to the park for quite a good number of days. School and homework must be keeping her occupied, I tried to reason out. But I was beginning to feel increasingly disappointed on each passing day. It was an inexplicable attachment on my part for the little mystery girl and her absence disturbed me.

She returned nearly after a month. I saw her sitting on the bench in the familiar posture, her eyes fixed at some invisible point close to the main entrance of the park. I was beginning to lose hope of seeing her again and her return had filled me with happiness. I went over to the bench and sat beside her. 'Where had you been all these days? Were you sick?' I asked.

She shook her head.

'Examinations going on?'

She nodded her head in reply.

I took out my phone and adjusted the camera, 'Would you mind if I take a snap?

She eyed me uncertainly but did not refuse. I took a couple of clicks. I zoomed the pictures and looked closely at them. They had come out nicely. The girl looked like a tiny angel. It would have been more lovely had she smiled a little. I could see a faint mud stain on the lower part of her pink frock. I turned and looked at the lower part of her frock. There was a distinct stain of mud or may be dirt on it. I wondered why her mother had not washed it. Mothers happen to be very keen about keeping the clothes of their children clean. But I did not ask her anything. She would perhaps not have given a proper reply to that, I guessed ruefully. 'I will get you a big chocolate tomorrow,' I said. 'Will you come here tomorrow?' I looked expectantly at her. She got down from the bench and headed into the interior of the park. I too stood up and walked after her keeping a good distance between us.

Then I heard it.

It was so small a sound that I thought it to be a figment of my imagination. A soft, delicate tinkling sound. I let my eyes sweep past the surroundings to detect the source of the sound. Nothing, nowhere! Suddenly it struck me, the sound was coming from the girl's feet. The tiny bells of her anklets produced that delicate tinkling. I wondered how come I had not heard it the day I had followed the girl to the inside of the park when she went to stand by the flowering bushes with some other children. I must have heard it but had ignored, or she might not have worn it that day, I thought.

I moved a bit closer and glanced at the girl's feet. There was a thin bangle like anklet on her left foot. Tiny bells dangled from it making a soft chime as she walked. My gaze travelled to the other foot, and I was shocked to find that there was no anklet around it. How could it be that she was wearing only one anklet? Where was the other one? I wanted to ask her if she had lost it somewhere. But my phone rang at that moment distracting my attention. I took the call and by the time the conversation was over the girl had disappeared out of sight.

The next day I went for jogging a little earlier than my usual time. I had made up my mind to ask her about the missing anklet and waited for her. She was not on the bench near the main entrance of the park. She might not come today, or she is somewhere inside the park, I thought and looked about here and there. I sauntered towards the inside of the park. Not many people were there at that early hour. Some youngsters were working out in the small gym, and a few elderly people were walking on the cemented track. Disappointed, I turned back thinking that she would perhaps come later or might not come at all.

There she was!

Not on the bench but on a swing little away from it. She was not sitting stiff as she usually did but was dangling her feet. The tiny bells of her single anklet tinkled like the soft musical notes. My heart leaped at the sight of her. I walked over to her and stood there leaning against the iron post of the swing. She stopped dangling her feet and looked at me.

'Can I sit here, on the swing?' I asked.

She nodded her head in reply.

I sat down and shifted closer to her. The swing moved a bit as I did so.

'Why are you wearing only one anklet? Where is the other one?'

'The girl gave me a searching glance, as if she were not sure whether to trust me or not.

'It is lost.' There was a deep sadness in her voice.

'Do you like the anklets a lot?'

'Yes, Papa gave me those on my birthday.'

I was feeling more and more excited. I had been seeing the girl for so many months, but she had never talked with me like the way she did that morning.

'How did you lose it? Did it fall somewhere while you played?'

'I lost it the night the storm came. I was sleeping. It was gone when I woke up.'

'How could that happen? It must have fallen in the bed or in the room.' I was getting a bit puzzled. It was a strange way to lose one's anklet. Her parents must have searched and failed to find it. How is it possible that a piece of ornament will be lost inside the house and is never recovered?

'It must have got entangled in the bedspread and later when the bedspread was washed it must have flown away along with the water. That's why you couldn't find it.' I said, trying to use the logic more to convince myself than her.

'I was not sleeping in the bed?'

I looked sharply at her.

'You were not sleeping in the bed, in a stormy night?' I was even more puzzled.

She did not say anything.

'Where did you sleep?' I was not ready to give up.

'Oh, I slept under the staircase. I was scared.'

Which parents would let their child sleep under a staircase in a stormy night? It was all so weird!

'Where did your parents sleep?' I asked.

'I do not know,' she said and got down.

I did not say anything. She looked at me for a brief moment and walked away.

The anklet was lost in a mysterious way. I could not work out any logical inference out of what the girl said. A small doubt nagged at my mind as I walked back home. Her unusual quietness, her reservations, and the glazed look in her eyes made her different from other children of her age. Could it be so that the girl was a bit sick in the head? There could not be any other plausible explanation for her abnormal behaviour. A sick mind can imagine many absurd things. That might be the reason why she loved to sit alone, avoided the company of others and invented tales about a stormy night and the missing anklet. At that point of time, it was the only possibility that explained her aloofness. I was deeply disturbed. I wondered what kind of unconcerned and careless parents could have let their mentally disoriented child to roam alone in a public park. 'I must meet her parents or the older member of her family who accompanies her to the park tomorrow and speak about this,' I decided before I reached back home.

But the girl did not come the next day and many more days after that. In the mean while I got my transfer order to my hometown. I had been sending representations to the authorities requesting for a transfer to my native place on the ground of my parent's ill health. I was advised to continue for a year at Maharastra since a transfer of an employee could not be done as per the official guidelines before he or she completed at least a year of service at the place of her first posting. Fortunately, they had considered my case sympathetically and complied to my appeal.

My parents were both happy and sad at the same time. Both of them had developed their individual circles with like-minded persons in the short span of just one year. But, as most of us, they too are emotionally linked to their native place. After all we have our roots there. So, the transfer came as a welcome change for all three of us.

Kusum auntie as well as the other neighbours were not happy about it. 'I am going to miss you a lot, 'Kusum auntie said sadly. 'We too will miss you and your delicious dishes,' Ma and Papa said. 'I will visit your place whenever I come here on official tour,' I said placatingly though I knew it was a remote possibility. 'We are not leaving immediately, I said to auntie, 'I have some pending assignments that would take me some time. Besides my substitute will not be joining till the end of the month. You can feed me with all your choice delicacies until that time.' I added with a broad smile. It did not bring a smile to Kusum auntie's face, though.

I longed to meet my mystery girl just once before I left Latur for good. But she never came again. Every morning I sat on the bench for while waiting for her to show up. And returned with a heavy, disappointed heart.

I found it more through an accident than by a chance.

It had rained a little the previous night. The jogging

path was wet and the grassy patches in it were squishy. There was some more time left for the dawn -break. The park lights were still on but the jogging path along its edge was partially dark. I jogged on listening to the music on my earphones. Suddenly I stumbled upon something hard and was pitched forward. It was sheer luck that I landed on my knees and palms instead of falling on my face. That could have been dangerous. I might have broken my teeth, or my nose or my face would have suffered a damage. I escaped only with some scratches on my palms and forearms and a slight sprain at my right ankle. What could have been the thing I stumbled upon? I tried to see and switched on the mobile phone light. I saw some object that was metallic and gray partially protruding out of the ground. I tried to pull it out, but it had gone deep inside. I looked around for a splinter of wood to dig it out. There was none. I took out the latch key of our front door from my pocket and tried to scrape out the earth from around the object. I succeeded after an effort of a few minutes. I could see the object now. It was something like a silver bangle. I hooked my finger under its rim and wrenched it out of the ground.

I held it up in my hand and looked closely at it.

It was a small silver anklet! Just like the one the girl wore! I do not know why but my palms felt moist. Was this one the missing anklet of Anjli? How did it reach this place? The way it was buried in the ground I could guess that it had been there for quite a long time. Why I, amongst all the people, had to chance upon it? I felt a bit spooked. I put the anklet in my pocket and strode back home. 'Anjli will be happy to get back her missing anklet. She is probably very fond of them and has not let anyone to take the other one of the pair out from her foot.' I thought.

I could not wait to see the sparkle of happiness in her big eyes as I gave her the anklet.

I waited for more than a week.

She did not come.

I was losing patience. We will be leaving this city in less than a couple of weeks. How shall I return her the anklet? I lay in the bed through a sleepless night wreaking my brain over the problem. Driven by an impulse, I selected a comparatively clear photo of Anjli from the ones I had taken in the park, superimposed the picture of the anklet on it and uploaded the photo on my social media site, captioning it as 'The Missing Anklet' and distantly hoping that someone of her family would come across it by some chance.

I had nothing else to do but wait.

I came across the comment day after the next.

'Want to talk to you urgently about the picture of the girl and the anklet you have posted. Please share your contact no.'

I was filled with a sudden enthusiasm. Finally, I have discovered someone of Anjli's family. But I did not want to post my phone number on a public site.

'Can't share my no. on the social media site. You can give me your number if you think if you need to talk to me urgently.' I wrote my comment.

The person posted the contact number without any objection.

I decided to make the call in the night. I was feeling excited and nibbled at my dinner. Mother eyed me in concern. 'Why aren't you eating properly, dear? Aren't you okay?'

'I am fine Ma, just not hungry tonight. Had some snacks at the office.' I lied and came to my room.

I closed the door and sat down on the bed. Oscillating between anxiety and inquisitiveness I rang the number on my phone and held it to my ear listening to the burr...burr at the other end.

'Hello.' An elderly male voice answered.

'You wanted to speak to me about a photo I had posted.' I said feeling ill at ease.

'Yes. I want to know how did you get the photo and where did you find the anklet?'

'Is the girl in the photo related to you in any manner?' I asked without answering his question.

'She was my daughter, Anjli.' The voice at the other end seemed to quiver.

'Was? You mean she is your daughter.' I was feeling slightly edgy now.

'She was my daughter. The anklet was hers, too. We have lost her years ago, in the earthquake. I would be greatly obliged to you if you courier the anklet to us. '

My throat had gone dry. My palms were clammy. The phone slipped out of my grip. I picked it up with a trembling hand.

'H..how did it happen?' I asked. My own voice sounded hoarse to me.

'It happened when we were at Latur, nearly three decades ago. We lived in the upper floor of a two storied building, I , my wife, my daughter Anjli and my son Anish. Another family stayed at the ground floor. The tremors happened at about four in the morning. We were all in deep slumber. The loud noise startled us. The lights had gone out. I picked up Anish and my wife pulled Anjli out of bed. We ran out of the door blindly groping for our way in the darkness. I do not know when Anjli's hand slipped out of my wife's. We ran down the flight of stairs. Just as we stepped on the first landing the staircase gave way under our feet with a loud crash. We were all thrown out. It was difficult to find one another in the clouds of dust. After a long time that appeared like a century, we were lifted up from under the heap of the ruined buildings by the rescue team. Anjli was missing. The rescue team searched under the debris for the missing people. A number of men women and children were buried under the rubbles. Some were alive, some were dead, and some were dying. But Anjli was never found. She must have been buried deep under the earth and that was why the rescue team failed to get her. We have moved off the place and are now settled at Nasik.' He took a deep breath.

'Please note down my address.' He resumed. 'I will be grateful to you forever if I could get back my daughter's anklet. You may value it as a cheap piece of jewelry but to me and my wife it will be a priceless relic of my daughter,' his voice broke towards the last.

I picked up a notebook and wrote down the address and assured him that I will send him his daughter's anklet by courier the next day. He thanked me and broke the connection.

I could not sleep for a long time. It was not possible to believe that the little girl I met in the park was the one the man spoke about. No amount of reasoning could convince me that the girl I spoke to, the girl I sat by on the swing and the girl whose pictures I had taken did not exist in actuality!

I did not go for jogging the next morning. I broke the routine after a long, long time. Mother was worried. 'Are you okay, dear? Why didn't you go to the park this morning?'

'It's nothing Ma. I worked on my laptop till late last night. You know I have to wind up certain work assignments before getting relieved. I woke up late in the morning. That's it.'

We were to leave the place two days after. I had engaged the Movers and Packers packing services to do the packing. Since the day I spoke to the person who introduced himself as Anjli's father, I avoided going to the park before it was day light and reasonably peopled. My eyes instinctively travelled to the bench and the swing where the girl used to sit. But they remained vacant.

It was our last day at the place. The furniture and other home appliances were getting loaded in the truck. We would start after the truck departed. Kusum auntie had invited us for lunch at her house. We surely would miss Kusum auntie and her hospitality. The truck left at about midday. My parents were at Kusum auntie's house. The house we had lived in for about a year looked empty and desolate now. I had developed an attachment towards the apartment in the past one year. It hurt to leave the place, but the thought of going back to our hometown did help a lot to overcome the sense of loss. There was still some time left time for the lunch. On a last-minute impulse I decided to take a look at the park. There would be no exercisers or joggers at the park at this time. I felt a bit uncertain, though. Yet I could not resist the temptation to make a visit there. I walked in through the main entrance and gazed around. The park was almost noiseless and empty except for a couple of security guards who sat gossiping on a bench to the left of the entrance. I sat down on a bench for a few minutes sipping in the cool silence. 'I won't be coming here again,' I thought nostalgically. I breathed out a deep sigh and rose to my feet.

I heard it then.

It was so soft at first that I took it to be the buzzing of some insect. Then it became more distinct. The delicate tinkling of bells! Just like the tinkling of Anjli's ankles! My heart gave a start. I looked at the bench to my left. The security guards were not there. Was I alone in the park? I walked fast towards the entrance. The sound grew a bit louder. I stopped at the entrance and compelled by an irrepressible urge I turned on my feet and glanced at the swing towards the right.

She sat on the swing and dangled her little legs. The swing moved gently under the impact. She wore the same mud-stained pink frock which she was wearing all those days I met her. My eyes travelled to her feet. Both her feet were adorned with the bangle shaped silver anklets. The tiny bells tinkled as she swung her legs to-and-fro. I stood transfixed, my unblinking eyes riveting on her. I wanted to walk out of the park, but my legs felt stiff.

She climbed off the swing slowly and walked towards the depth of the park. My eyes followed her. She reached the bend by a big flowering shrub and turned.

There was an enchanting, angelic smile on her face.

It was the most beautiful and most enigmatic thing I had ever seen.

A lone bird flapped its wings on a tree startling me. For a fraction of a moment my eyes turned towards the tree.

I looked again at the bend by the flowering bush.

She was gone!

*****

The Dressing Table

The pick-up van revved noisily as it made its way through the wooden gate.

Anu, driven by curiosity wandered to the window to see why the vehicle had entered their compound in that hot April midday. Her curiosity turned to surprise as she saw Binay, her husband walking ahead of the pickup van directing the driver towards the front veranda of their small asbestos topped house. She opened the front door and came out.

Her husband looked at her, a sparkle of joy flickering in his eyes.

Anu's eyes travelled to the thing that stood in the van. It was a dressing table, fitted with ornately designed drawers on either side. The big mirror was covered with several layers of old newspapers which were tied up across the glass carefully.

'At last, ' Binaya said with a smile, 'your wish is fulfilled.'

'It is a dressing table, isn't it? So, we have one finally!'

Anu responded the smile, feeling secretly delighted.

At last! Yes, at last her long suppressed wish of owning a dressing table was fulfilled.

Anu came from family that was not financially very well off. Her father was a low paid employee in a government office and it was quite an effort to provide a comfortable living to his family of ten members. He had his old parents who needed looking after, six children who needed good food and good education. Tried as he might it was an impossible task to make all the odd ends meet. Overworking had made him look old and gnarled even at a young age. But he sent Anu, the eldest of his children and the other five, three daughters and two sons, to good schools despite the financial constraints. He wanted his children to grow up in a good academic environment. It was however not possible to provide them with the comforts and luxury the children of rich families enjoyed. They had to manage with only the bare minimum, be it clothes or food.

Anu was a beautiful girl. Her school friends said so. With a complexion that had a wheatih translucence and a chiselled face with a sharp nose, well-shaped arched eyebrows, large liquid eyes and full lips she stood out amongst others.

'God has designed you in His sweet leisure,'

Rina, her friend remarked often.

Every day, as she got ready for the school, she looked at herself in the blotchy mirror that hung on the wall of the narrow dining space. She could not see anything special in the face of the girl that looked back at her from the small mirror. Why do they say that she was beautiful, she wondered.

It was the last year in school. The school final

examination was a month or so away. On the occasion of Saraswati puja Anu and her friends decided to go to a movie. It was their last puja in the school. No one knew if there would be any such occasion in future when all the friends would be together. Anu did not have much difficulty in obtaining her father's permission since her friend Nira advocated for her. It was decided that the girls would assemble at Rina's house and from there they would go to the movie hall.

They sat together gossiping and giggling in Rina's spacious, tastefully furnished room.

Anu's gaze was riveted on the dressing table that stood by the window its big mirror draped by a cotton screen that hung from a drawstring.

Rina entered the room with a plate of fruits and sweets and put it on the bed. 'Let's have some fruits and then we will set out for the cinema hall.'

They ate the sweets and fruits amidst chatting and laughter. Rina went over to the dressing table and drew back the cotton screen revealing the spotless shiny mirror.

She took out a powder box, a face cream, and a comb from the drawer and called, 'Come on girls, let's give ourselves a touch up before we start'. They got up from the bed and walked to the dressing table. Nira stood in front of the mirror examining her full length image the mirror reflected. Others followed suit . They applied cream and powder to their faces and appraised their looks. Anu was the last to stand in front of the mirror. She marvelled at the sight of the big polished mirror. Gingerly, she studied her image in it. A lovely girl in a cheap cotton salwar suit of pink stood facing her, a look of puzzlement in her big dark eyes. It was so different from the girl she met every day in the blotchy mirror that hung on the cracked wall of their dining space. Given the choice and the freedom Anu would have kept standing there in front of the mirror for hours.

'How long are you going to admire yourself my beauty?' Lipi teased. ' We will be late for the movie.

Anu blushed and turned away from the mirror. But all the time she was watching the movie her thoughts kept returning to the dressing table and the full-length mirror.

A week or so later Anu mustered up courage to speak to her father. That evening when her father sat relaxed sipping tea from a steaming cup, Anu walked up to him. She stood quietly waiting for her father to finish the tea.

'What is it dear? Do you want to say something?' He asked fondly.

'Father! Let's buy a dressing table' She blurted out without a preamble.

'Dressing table?' Her father looked at her in surprise. 'What on earth for?'

Anu could not think of any convincing answer. She stood quite drawing imaginary half circles on the cement floor with her toe nail.

'Better you take more interest in you studies instead of getting distracted in this manner. Your school finals is round the corner.'

Her father said shortly and got up from the chair.

Anu was not a bright student. Putting in all her serious efforts she managed to secure only average marks. She shouldn't have approached father with such an absurd proposition at a time when her focus should have been on her studies, Anu thought guiltily. Her mother came out and ran a loving hand through her hair.

'A dressing table? We will give you one as your bridal-gift,' she said, a small smile hovering on her face.

Anu did not say anything and walked inside.

Despite all her hard work Anu managed to secure just pass mark in the final examination.

Somehow, she got a seat in a private college and continued her studies. Soon after the completion of higher secondary she was married to Binay , a clerk in a government office. The marriage ceremony was a simple affair. Anu's parents spent according to what their financial condition permitted. But they could not include a dressing table in the list of her bridal gifts.

Binay was an affectionate person. He had no bad habits and tried his best to keep Anu happy.

Anu held no grievance against him. She considered herself lucky to have got an innocent man like Binay as her life partner.

Time and again the dressing table in Rina's room haunted her. Her longing used to grow stronger when she saw one in the house of her neighbours or relatives. But she had learnt to keep her wishes unexpressed.

One night, in an intimate moment with Binay she gave her wish a voice.

'Can we buy a dressing table?'

'A dressing table? Why, sure! There will be a raise in my salary in a few months. We will buy one,' he assured.

Anu had not thought that Binay would agree so readily. Her heart was filled with love and gratitude for him. But her life changed after a few months She conceived her first child, her son Bijoy.

And in the following years came another son and a daughter. Her life was so full of happiness as well as responsibilities with their arrival that the dressing table was forgotten like a distant dream.

And years rolled by. The family responsibilities kept her so preoccupied that she could not think of anything beyond that. Her children grew up. The eldest Bijoy now was doing his MCA in a college at Cuttack. Her second son had completed his graduation and the daughter was studying plus two in a junior college. She was beginning to feel a little less stressed even though the household chores kept her busy most part of the day. In all these years Anu had not found enough time to look at herself closely in the old 8»×10» mirror in her bedroom.

But she had not given it much thought. Nor was she any longer interested in the self-appraisal of her looks. It was only a few days before when her young daughter mentioned about it, the dressing table came back to her thoughts.

'Mama, tell Baba to bring a dressing table. Most of my friends have one in their house.'

It was as if a young Anu was speaking out in her daughter's voice.

That night she had told Binay about her daughter's wish. And Binay remembered.

He recalled a night long many years ago when his young bride had expressed her wish to buy a dressing table.

But life has been so demanding in the meanwhile that the dressing table was completely erased from his mind.

He had decided to give his wife a surprise Without letting her know he had ordered a beautifully designed dressing table. It was an expensive affair but was nothing compared to the joy that sparkled in the eyes of his wife.

Her daughter returned from college in the afternoon. Her excitement at the sight of the new dressing table was beyond words.

'You are a darling, mama,' she said entwining her arms around Anu's neck. I knew you could convince father as no one would.

Her father's face lit up with a fond smile.

'You are right my dear, but this time I got a bit late in fulfilling your mother's wish.'

Anu laughed.

The dressing table stood tall and shiny in their bedroom. Her daughter sat on the stool facing the mirror doing her hair. She would not budge off her place in spite of Anu's warnings that she was getting late for her coaching class. At last, with much reluctance she came out of the room and went out to attend the class. Binay had already gone to the place of one of his colleagues to discuss some office matter. Anu was alone in the house.

She could not bring herself to go close to the dressing table. It was as if the fragile thing would fall apart even at a close look from her. She was torn between an overwhelming urge to look at herself in the mirror and a fear that something ominous might happen now that her long nourished dream had been realized.

She looked furtively around. Bo one was there. No one watched her through the window.

Slowly, carefully, as if the dressing table will disappear at the noise of her footfall she walked up to the table and looked into the mirror.

A middle-aged woman with a drawn bony face stared back at her from the mirror. The receding hairline, the greying clumps at the temples, the dull, shrunken eyes and the puckered lips made her a complete stranger. It was not so that Anu had not seen herself in the mirror all these years, but the change in her appearance had never been so boldly pronounced. The beautiful girl with a chiselled face and long, silk tresses she had met in the mirror at Rina's house in that Saraswati puja had long since disappeared somewhere in the dark recess of time. This haggard, frail woman did not retain even a faint semblance of that girl. She moved away from the dressing table and draped the mirror with a bedsheet.

'' Let's get the dressing table shifted to our daughter's room, 'she said to Binay that night.

'Why? Binay looked surprised. 'You had always wanted a dressing table.'

'I don't need a dressing table at this age. She needs it. ' Anu smiled briefly.

'May be, I will meet girl in the pink salwar suit who loved to look at herself in the mirror in her.' She thought and turned her face away.

*****

A Defeated Dream

A crowd of students stood in the corridor staring anxiously at the closed door of room number 17 of the New Boys' Hostel. Two police constables were trying to break open the lock. A swarm of media people has arrived in the meanwhile. The police inspector barked admonitions to keep away from the place. The door was opened after a while. All eyes rivetted on the body hanging from the fan hook. It looked grotesque, the tongue protruding out, eyes bulging and hands and legs hanging stiff. Two policemen took the body off and laid it down on the floor. The parents wailed loudly and tried to push their ways through the mass of students and cameramen. The police held them back with much effort. The young, handsome and brilliant Abhimanyu now lay on the floor, ugly and lifeless. The blaring ambulance cruised up to the hostel gate. Two uniformed men got down with a stretcher, lifted Abhimanyu on to it and carried the stretcher to the waiting vehicle.

As the ambulance made its way through the gates Abhimanyu's parents ran after it, howling in grief, and then scrambled into their car that followed the ambulance. The media persons were still busy collecting bytes from the students and inmates of the New Boys' Hostel. The information they gathered were mostly based on guesses and speculations rather than elements of truth. But neither they nor the boys who wanted to see themselves on the TV screen were tired of the process. The policemen locked and sealed the door of room number 17, and asked the students and other spectators to leave the place. Slowly the crowd dispersed amidst fading noises and indistinct conversations. A ghostly silence descended on the deserted corridor.

+ +   ++   ++   ++   ++

They all eagerly waited for the teacher. It was their first day in the Government High School. They came from different schools but most of them had secured good marks in the board examination. Their young minds were bursting with excitement and ambition at the prospect of studying in one of the best schools. They talked about their earlier experiences in their old schools, their teachers, the games they used to play and so many such things. Two boys who stood on the veranda in front of the classroom hurried inside .'The Head Master is coming here,' they announced.

Suddenly there was total silence in the classroom. The Head Master strode in with an air of dignity. They all stood up.

'Good morning, sir, ' they said in unison and greeted him.

'Good morning, students. Sit down.'

They all sat down and looked expectantly at the Head Master.

'You are now in the High School. This is here your future is going to be shaped. You have to have a specific aim in your life and prepare yourself accordingly. The teachers here will give you proper guidance no doubt, but you must have a clear vision of what you are going to pursue. Do you get me?'

'Yes sir,' the answer came in a chorus.

'Good. So now tell me each one of you what is your aim in life and how you are going to prepare yourself for achieving it in the next three years here.'

Most of the boys and girls particularly sitting in the front benches said that they would be doctors. Some others aimed at being engineers and teachers. Abhimanyu sat silently in the last but one bench.

The Head Master wandered close to where he sat.

'Don't you have any aim? Why do you sit in silence?'

Abhimanyu rose to his feet. 'I too want to be a doctor sir. But I don't know if I can fulfil my aim. '

'If I am not mistaken you have scored ninety eight percent in the board examination. Why do you lack confidence?'

Abhimanyu did not say anything.

"Remember students ' the Head Master said, turning to look at others. 'It is good to be humble. But never let your humility get over your convictions,' He patted Abhimanyu's back and walked up to the table.

++ ++   ++ ++   ++ ++

Abhimanyu stood shyly facing the camera. The news reporters were asking him so many questions at one time and he felt extremely embarrassed. He looked at his father's face. He glowed with pride. Tears of joy brimmed in his mother's eyes. All the media people were asking him the same question his Head Master had asked five years ago....'What is your aim in life? What would you want to be?'

'You have secured the second position among the best twenty in the council examination. What would you like to be in future? A news reporter, who seemed to be more demanding than others brought the boom very close to Abhimanyu's face and asked.

'A doctor!' Abhimanyu said slowly and turned his face away from the camera.

It was an evening of celebration in Abhimanyu's house. There was a rushing inflow of friends and relatives to their house. All of them congratulated him and wished him best for a better career.

Abhimanyu felt elated. He had laboured hard all through and God had rewarded him. He was overwhelmed with a sense of gratitude towards the Almighty and also to his parents who had extended all possible supports to him. But the going was still difficult. He had to clear the medical entrance with a good percentile before getting the dream realized. God was kind and generous, it seemed. He got through the National Eligibility cum Entrance Test with exceptionally good rank and got a seat in one of the best medical colleges.

The time came to say goodbye to his hometown and to his parents. Mother wept and father looked worried and apprehensive. They had never let Abhimanyu out of their sight. They were anxious how he would live alone in an unknown environment and amidst strangers. But despite their anxieties and concerns they were excited about the bright future of their son. He was going to pass out from a renowned medical college and would do higher studies in some specialized branch of medical science. And so, Abhimanyu set out to fulfil the ambition he had nurtured since his school days.

+   +   +   +   +   +   +

His immediate reaction at the first sight of the massive and majestic structure was one of awe and reverence. He could not believe he was going to live a new life in this ambience. Most of the first-year students reacted in the same way as Abhimanyu did. It did not take much time for them to get introduced to one another and even make friends. The boy Abhimanyu liked at the first sight was Varun, a boy who came from a small town like him. Like Abhimanyu Varun too was given a single room in the New Boys' Hostel. All of them were happy about their future prospects.

++ ++ ++   ++ ++ ++ ++ ++ ++

They all had gathered in the huge hall to attend the orientation class. Everyone looked expectantly at the massive portals, waiting to see it open and the teachers enter.

The big doors opened a few minutes after and the Dean of the college brisked in, followed by a group of professors, exuding an aura of knowledge and grandeur. They stood up. To Abhimanyu it was a dèjàvu....an action replay of his first day at the High School, the Head Master entering the class and greeting them.

'Good morning students, ' the Dean addressed them in a deep, sonorous voice.

'You should feel proud that you have got entry to this famous college. You all know that to treat the sick is the noblest act in the Lord's world. That was the reason doctors are believed to be the ones next to God. A doctor should be honest to his profession because he is the God's chosen one, the one assigned with the duty of saving lives. You are all brilliant students. You must labour hard to attain your goal, be genuine in your approach and never compromising. I hope you all have got my point. Haven't you?'

'Yes, sir ' the reply was loud and unanimous.

Then they introduced themselves to the Dean and the professors. Abhimanyu had started enjoying the ambience.

It was after two by the time the orientation class was over. They were feeling hungry and walked to the dining hall. Abhimanyu sat with Varun and Sohan. They chatted on several things while they ate. 'Food is good here,' Sohan said. 'Yes, I don't think I would miss much my mother's cooking here.' Varun added and smiled. Abhimanyu too smiled relishing the food as well as the conversation.

'Let's enjoy as much as we can,' Sohan said. ' The classes would start tomorrow and the seniors would be back here. God knows what they are going to do to us.'

'But ragging is forbidden in educational institutions now. How could they rag us?' Abhimanyu asked, suddenly losing interest in the food.

'They would, buddy. I have heard from my brother that in some technical colleges the ragging is very nasty.'

'Then we must protest. Ragging is illegal,' Abhimanyu persisted. Sohan let out a derisive laughter. 'They care two hoots for your so-called law. Some of them come from families of top political leaders who can easily twist the law with their little fingers to their own convenience. And you are talking of protest...huh!'

They walked over to their rooms. 'Let's hope things do not get too difficult for us,' Varun said and went to his room. Abhimanyu unlocked the door of room no 17, went inside and shut it. He put the suitcases on the bed and began unpacking. He was done within an hour. He changed the bedspread and pillow cover and lay down. He was exhausted from the day's heavy engagements but sleep was far away from his eyes. He was torn with a mixed up feeling of excitement, expectation, and apprehension.

+ + + + + + + + +

Abhimanyu walked down the corridor. It was lunch break. The corridor was not very crowded though. He heard the tapping sound of high heel shoes behind and turned. A girl was walking just a little behind him. She wore a salwar suit and a sling bag hung from her shoulder. Abhimanyu recalled that she was sitting on the front bench in the class. 'She must be a new entry to the college like him,' he decided and smiled at the girl.

'Hi, are you in first year?'

'Yes, and you?'

'I am in first year too. I am Abhimanyu.'

'Amisha,' the girl said. 'How do you find the atmosphere here?'

'Academic and serious but I like it that way.,'

They walked along making small talks about their hometowns, colleges and their parents. Abhimanyu was feeling comfortable in the company of Amisha.

Three boys were sitting on the balustrade. They were smoking cigarettes. A boy shoved his leg forward obstructing the way. Abhimanyu stopped on his track. 'Hey, wait.'

'First year? Both of you?' Another boy asked showing his yellowing teeth in an ugly grin. Abhimanyu saw from the corner of his eyes a couple of girls in tops and jeans, and a few more boys approaching them. He was filled with misgivings.

'Yes' he said trying to sound polite.

'He felt the sharp sting of the slap on his right cheek before he could identify which one of them was closing in on him.

'It is yes *sir*!, you dumb ass,' he said menacingly. 'Got it?'

'Yes sir,' Abhimanyu said in a whisper.

'Louder, ' the boy in the red T shirt demanded and slapped him again. Yes, sir, '

Abhimanyu said loudly.

'Give your hair a crew cut. Henceforth wear only white shirts and trousers. And say 'good morning, sir or good afternoon' to greet us every time you meet us. Is that understood?'

The two girls came closer to Amisha. One of them pulled at the stole Amisha wore.

'Hey Behan ji! I like your hair style. Show me how you did it....

One of the senior girls pulled Anisha's long braid and tried to untwine it. The other one gripped her hand so hard that the thick glass bangle broke.

'Hey sister, ' one of the boys jeered. Do you dance? Come on, show us some dancing.. and you, dude' He turned to look at Abhimanyu, 'do fifty sit-ups. Quick!

Amisha stood helplessly, her eyes heavy with tears of humiliation.

'Didn't you hear what he said?' The senior girl snapped at her. 'Start dancing!' Abhimanyu looked from the corners of his eyes. Other senior boys were beginning to wander in.

'I will do the sit-ups sir,' he blurted out loudly 'Please leave the girl alone.'

The senior boys looked at one another. They seemed to be thoroughly amused. 'Hey Yash, did you hear what this nincompoop said? He says to leave the girl alone.'

The boy whose name was Yash laughed loudly. 'Okay, dude, trying to be chivalrous, huh?

Then you perform her share of the act. Hey girls! Someone get a sari for him. He will perform in costume.'

They pulled both of them to a classroom that was empty. Another senior girl brought in a sari. 'Take off your shirt,' Yash commanded. 'This is not fair,' Abhimanyu protested, summoning up courage. 'You can't do this to me. Ragging is against law,'

'Is it? Hey listen you all. He is teaching us law. It is not a law college, buddy. *Our* law prevails here. So be a good boy and take off your shirt.' Another boy who called himself Dilip slapped Abhimanyu so hard that his ears burnt and his head began to spin. Yash and another boy tucked the border of the sari in to his pant and wrapped it clumsily around his waist. The senior girls helped him to do the pleats. They passed the sari over his shoulder and draped it over his head. Someone made a red dot like spot on his forehead with a lipstick.

'Put some lipstick on his lips too. He will look beautiful.' A boy said looking at the girls. One of them picked out another lipstick from her big vanity bag and dabbed the stick on his lips.

'He looks good now. Start the performance. Hey, somebody play a song.'

One of the boys played a song on his cell phone. 'Come on, dance!'

There was no way to escape. Abhimanyu moved his legs and hands to the beat of the song.

'Don't you have life in you? Dance faster!' Yash shouted.

Amisha ran away from the place crying loudly. Abhimanyu tried to move his feet faster but they felt like stone. Yash pulled a punch at his face. Abhimanyu lost balance and fell down. Dilip and another boy who wore a beard kicked at him. 'This is for today, Mr. doctor-lawyer,' he said. 'We will meet tomorrow' they went away laughing their raucous laughter.

Varun knocked gently at the door of room.17 and waited. The door didn't open.

He knocked again and called...'Abhimanyu, please

open the door.' Abhimanyu dragged himself out of the bed and opened the door. Varun was shocked at Abhimanyu's sight. His eyes were swollen. Under his right eye there was a blood bruise. There was a still a faint stain of lipstick on his lips.

'My God, Abhimanyu, what have they done to you? What did you do to provoke this outrage?'

'They were troubling a girl. One of them slapped me. I just pointed out that ragging is not legal. That's all.'

'That has triggered their anger, I presume. They asked me to take off my shirt and trousers and do a few dance steps. But they have warned me to attend the ragging class regularly at nine every evening.'

'I had no idea they could be so cruel. I am going to complain to the Dean.'

'Don't even think of doing that.' Varun cautioned him. 'That will make them even more angry. The Dean won't provide you a security guard who will be with you twenty four hours to protect you.'

Abhimanyu thought for a while. 'Ok. If you say so... this time I am not complaining but I sure will bring it to his notice if they again torture me like this.'

They went to the dining hall. It was an effort to munch the food with the swollen jaw but Abhimanyu managed to eat something. He wanted to keep his energy on level. Some senior boys sauntered in, laughing and talking in a loud voice. One of them turned to look at them ....

'Already got stamped, huh!! ' He jeered looking at Abhimanyu's bruised face. He had a laughter that sounded like the neighing of a horse. Another one walked close to the table where Varun and Abhimanyu sat eating. 'Carry on doctors, but do not forget to be regular in the ragging class. It starts from tomorrow night. Got that?'

'Yes sir,' Varun replied before Abhimanyu could say anything.

'Good'. The boy who had a neighing laughter said and strode away with his friends.

'How can they be so inhuman, so nasty in their behaviour? Aren't they supposed to be future doctors?'

Abhimanyu said as they reached Varun's room. Varun wished him good night and went in. Abhimanyu entered his room and locked the door from inside.

He was feeling thoroughly drained out and was asleep as soon as he lay on the bed.

A series of loud bangs on his door jerked him out of sleep. 'Open up, fresher..'

Scared, but not panicked, Abhimanyu opened the door. Yash, Dilip and two others barged in. They closed the door behind them and looked at Abhimanyu. 'So, ragging is illegal, isn't that what you said?'

Yash demanded. 'I am sorry about that sir,' Abhimanyu blurted trying to cool the seniors.

'We do not need your sorry, boy. You have to be punished.' Dilip sneered. The four senior boys took off their shirts and shorts and threw them at Abhimanyu.' Wash them clean, now!' A senior boy ordered.

Abhimanyu stared at them in disbelief. He had never washed his own clothes while at home. Mother would never let him. Tears of distress rolled out his eyes. 'Store those precious pearls for other occasions, buddy. There will be many more.'

'I can't wash clothes, sir!' He mumbled.

'You can. Put them in the bucket add water and detergent powder. Then rub and beat them and wash a few times with fresh water.'

Abhimanyu didn't move.

Dilip grabbed his hand and took off his shirt. He repeated the same performance with his shorts. He was now only in his underwear.'

'Too many clothes will hinder your work. Now go and wash them.'

Abhimanyu staggered into the bathroom. He opened the tap. Then put the dirty jeans, socks and shirts in the bucket and added detergent powder. Suppressing the overwhelming urge to protest with all the efforts it would take, he washed the clothes and rinsed them dry. He handed the clothes to the boys who sat on his bed, smoking.

'This will do for now. Go to sleep now. Tomorrow there will be more clothes for you.' They strode out of the room banging the door behind them.

Abhimanyu slumped on the bed, trembling. There was dirt on the bed and cigarette butts lay scattered here and there. He beat the dirt and dust off the bed with the help of a towel, cleaned the room and lay down on the bed. Sleep eluded him. He did not know what was going to happen to him, how he was going to survive this humiliation. He thought and wept. He was now sure that he would not tell anything about this to his parents. It would only add to their misery.

He asked Varun if the seniors had gone to his room too last night.

'They had come around eleven o' clock or so. Some boys asked me to massage their backs. I did as they said. They did not slap me this time. But I heard them knocking at the rooms of Goutam and Surjit'. I don't know exactly what happened.'

'How could they take a ragging class here when ragging is forbidden in educational institutions? Someone must report it to the authorities.'

'We have to bear with it for a few months. There will be no ragging in the second semester.' Varun sounded hopeful.

'It won't be easy to put up with this kind of torture for months. Someone must do something about it.'

That afternoon after the classes Abhimanyu called his classmates and requested them to stand up united against the senior boys and report the matter to the Dean in writing. Only four or five of the students agreed but the rest were too scared even to discuss the seniors.

Abhimanyu felt defeated. It needed a tremendous effort to put up with such physical and emotional harassment. But everyone seemed to have taken it for granted. He breathed out a deep sigh of frustration.

It was exactly nine in wall clock of the hall when Varun and Abhimanyu entered the big hall. Other first year students were arriving in groups and solo. They stood waiting for the senior boys, butterflies fluttering in their bellies and their hearts beating fast. Ten minutes past nine Yash, Romi, Karan and some senior girls walked in.

'Stand in rows boys and take off your dress. Be only in your underpants. The girls were asked to wear their hair loose and apply a thick layer of foundation cream on their faces. A senior girl student pulled hard at a fresher's plait of hair and she began to scream. Another senior girl came up with a pair of scissors and cut the plait at the middle. She repeated the performance with others who wore their hair in long plaits.

Someone played a song on the mobile phone.

'Dance and introduce yourselves while dancing.' Yash commanded.

All the first-year boys and girls began dancing to the beats of the song and shouted their introductions. The dancing went on for more than half an hour. They were warned again to wear white or cream coloured outfits and simple shoes and give their hair a crew cut. The girls were asked to wear simple salwar suits and hold their hair in a hair clip. 'No braids, ' a senior girl said. A boy called Ronit from first year whom Abhimanyu had not met earlier stood folding his hands in a pose of reverence even after the ragging class was declared over. Dilip walked up to him and patted his back. 'You are a good boy,' he said sounding glad. He seemed to have been moved by the boy's servility.

'Ok juniors, same place same time tomorrow!' The senior boys said and moved away filling the corridor with their boisterous laughter.

Nothing very significant happened for a week. Every evening at nine they would attend the ragging class. They were asked to do dancing, run errands like getting cigarettes and sandwiches and cold drinks for the seniors from the nearby stores. The girls were asked to sing and dance and carry out the orders of the seniors. Abhimanyu noticed that the seniors were not tough on Ronit. They exempted him from doing hard tasks. He discussed it with Varun. 'Forget him, the docile, tail-wagging cheapie. He has somehow satisfied the older boys with his servile gestures.'

Ronit and Sujoy were sitting at the table by the window. 'Hi!' Ronit greeted Abhimanyu and Varun smiling broadly. Abhimanyu did not smile. 'How could you be so unctuous?'

Abhimanyu asked. 'They are treating us like vermin. Should we not protest? They are getting the boost from boys like you. We can stand together against this abomination instead of licking at their leftovers.'

'*You* play the rebel buddy, 'Ronit said, sarcasm dripping off his words. 'We have no complaints to make against any one.' He looked at Sujoy who sat silently listening to the verbal battle between Abhimanyu and Ronit.

'Don't enter into any conflicts Abhi. Let's eat,' Varun pulled Abhimanyu away from the spot. 'Boys like you are responsible for what the seniors do to us.' Abhi spat at Ronit and strode after Varun.

The ambience of the hostel was beginning to appear calm and peacefully settled until one night Varun heard the loud bangs on the door of a room on his floor. He sat up groggily and squinted at his mobile phone. It showed eleven forty-two. 'Who could be banging at the door so loudly at this hour, he wondered. May be some boys had gone to watch a late-night movie and are banging the door of their room to wake up the roommate who was left behind.

He tried to go back to sleep. Then he heard a muffled scream. The voice sounded familiar. Abhimanyu ?? His heart skipped a beat then began to pound erratically. He got down from the bed and tiptoed to the door of his room. He unbolted it noiselessly and peeped out. His gaze turned sharply in the direction from which the screams were coming. Abhimanyu 's was room no 17, two rooms away from his own. The two rooms in between were unoccupied. Sohan and another boy were in the room at the far end of the corridor. Varun doubted if the boys in the other rooms have heard the soft screams. Maybe they were afraid to come out and inquire. He walked a few steps towards room no. 17 and pricked his ears to listen. He could only hear voices, indistinct and distant. Suddenly he noticed a movement of the door panel. Someone was opening the door from inside. He raced back to his room and bolted the door. He stood for a while leaning against the door, breathing hard. There was complete silence. His legs shaking badly, he walked to the bed and flopped down. He remained awake for a long time speculating what the senior boys might be doing in room no. 17. It was almost three in the morning by the time he slept.

He awoke with a jerk. As if someone had pulled him out of the bed. The sun hadn't risen yet. Everybody in the hostel were asleep. He came out of his room and tiptoed towards room no 17. He cast a furtive glance around to see if anyone was watching. The corridor looked deserted. He touched the door panel gingerly as if it would spring at him the moment he touched it. To his surprise the door panel shifted inside at his touch. The door was open!! He pushed the panel a little more and entered.

Abhimanyu lay on the floor, tucked in a sheet. His

face was swollen and badly bruised. Blood oozed from a large cut on the lower lip.

Varun sat by him, shocked and scared.

'Get me some water.' Abhimanyu moaned.

Varun ran to his room came back carrying a bottle of drinking water. He lifted Abhimanyu's head gently and made him drink a little. Abhimanyu stood up with a lot of effort and lurched to the bed. He lay down and began to whimper. Varun noticed the mark of cigarette burns on his chest and arms.

'This is monstrous!' Varun gasped. 'Why should they do all these to you? What have you done?'

'I have raised voice against ragging which none of you had the courage to do,' Abhimanyu said. His voice was a croaking whisper. ' I had no idea that my dream to become a doctor could be so demanding. Do they make doctors here? They forge devils. These devils will save human lives in future!! What a bloody joke!' Abhimanyu curled his aching lips in a sardonic smile.

'Who were they?'

'They were seven. I could recognise only Yash, Karan, Dilip, and Ranjit. Rest of them were strangers.'

'I will get your breakfast here. You need not get up. Take rest.' Varun said soothingly.

'I am beginning to think I should not be a doctor after all if I have to pay this price. I would rather go back to my parents and try for some other course,' Abhimanyu said more to himself than Varun. His gaze was fixed at some invisible spot on the ceiling.

'Don't lose heart buddy, ' Varun put his hand on Abhimanyu's shoulder. Things will be alright soon. '

'It will not change for me. It seems they are carrying a personal vendetta against me. They said they would again come tonight. They will never leave me alone. Someone has put it in their minds that I am going to the authorities to make a complaint. May be Ronit and Sujoy.'

'You are such a brilliant student. You will get over these initial hurdles with a little patience. Do not worry.' Varun consoled his friend and went out.

He saw Ronit and Sujoy coming out of their room. Ronit flashed him a crooked smile. Varun did not smile back and climbed down the stairs.

Abhimanyu was asleep when Varun reached room no. 17. He put the breakfast tray on the table and left without disturbing Abhimannyu.

Varun returned to the hostel at about six in the evening. Abhimanyu was still lying on the bed. But he was awake. The breakfast tray lay untouched. He turned to look at Varun. There was a look in Abhimanyu's eyes that troubled Varun.

'How are you feeling, Abhi?'

'Fine... I am fine. Do not worry about me.'

'Why haven't you eaten anything? Come let's have some snacks. I am hungry.' Varun wanted to cheer him up.

'I do not feel like eating anything. You go. I want to be alone for while.'

' You have been alone all day long,' Varun countered. ' You need some company now. Come to my room.'

'Please Varun. Let me be alone for some time' Abhimanyu said.

Varun could not resist the sincere urge in his voice. He walked out of the room closing the door behind him. He went to call him for dinner. The door was locked from inside. Varun rapped on the door and waited. Abhimanyu did not open the door.

'Hey Abhi, let's go down for dinner,'

'I do not need any dinner. You go and do not disturb me please,'

Disappointed, Varun went down to the dining hall alone. He met Goutam, Sohan, Anil and most of others there.

'Why isn't Abhimanyu here? I heard that they had gone to his room last night.... Karan, Yash and Dilip and other seniors. What did they do to him? Is he okay?'

Anil asked Varun in a hushed voice, looking concerned. 'Who told you about it?'

Varun asked, surprised.

'Ronit and Sujoy'

'So, Ronit knew it all along. The snooping wretch!! Abhimanyu had guessed right. It was Ronit who poisoned the minds of the seniors against him.

'He is sleeping perhaps. He did not open the door when I went to call him for dinner. I think he will come later.'

Abhimanyu's door was still shut when Varun returned to his own room. The corridor was empty. There was no sign of Ronit, Sujoy, Gautam and others. Varun got near the door of room no. 17. He was about to knock when a thought made him stop. 'Let him sleep over it. He will get back his composure tomorrow morning. O God, please let not the seniors trouble him again tonight. ' He prayed and went back to his room.

The commotion at early morning jolted him out of an uneasy sleep. He ran to the door and jerked it open. The inmates of the New Boys' Hostel had thronged outside Abhimanyu's room. He slid into a shirt and went to look, his heart in his mouth. The hostel warden and two other supervisors were rapping at the door loudly.

'Intimate the Dean, ' someone said. The Dean reached after fifteen minutes or so. A call was put through to the Police Station at his advice. Another fifteen minutes passed before the sirens of the police vehicles were heard. The police finally broke open the door and discovered Abhimanyu's body hanging from the fan hook in the ceiling. Overwhelmed with grief and fear Varun ran back to his room and shut the door. His eyes burned. He wanted to cry out loudly. But no sound came out of him. He sat on the floor, leaning to the door, trembling violently.

Long after the ambulance carrying the body had left, he heard a knock on the door of his room. He rose to his feet with an effort and opened the door. The two police men looked at him sympathetically. Later they asked him if he knew what exactly happened that compelled Abhimanyu to end his life. Varun answered the questions but he did not say that he knew the senior boys had come to Abhimanyu's room the other night. 'I did not know him closely. We have met here just a fortnight or so before. He did not confide in me,' he said. The policemen seemed to be convinced.

One of them took out a folded piece of paper from a zip-lock bag using a gloved hand and showed it to Varun. He straightened the paper and held it out before him.

'Is it Abhimanyu's writing?' He asked. Varun peered at the paper, shaken but curious. 'I am not sure. Can I take a closer look?' The police man brought the letter closer. The letter was written in a neat handwriting. But they looked somehow a little blurred. Varun took out a hanky from his pocket, wiped his burning eyes and let his gaze sweep over the lines.

'Dear Mama,

I won't be alive when this letter will reach you. Sorry to betray your and papa's expectations in me in this way. What must have I done, mama? I wanted to go back to you and papa. But then I thought why to add to your trouble? Like me you both also had dreamt that I would be a reputed doctor one day. I had laboured so hard to accomplish that goal. But I have now realized that you couldn't be a doctor just by being a good student or doing hard work. You have to put up with the monstrosity of people too and the biggest irony is that the monsters are future doctors. These future doctors had transformed my dream to a nightmare. You and papa had always asked me to be brave, but I have so pathetically failed you. I do not want to show my face to you people. I curse the day I had told the headmaster of the school that I wanted to be a doctor. What a ridiculous aim I had kept feeding on with all my perseverance and diligence! I want to keep writing to you mama........ but I can't. Mama I am being honest with you... I really do not want to be a doctor. Forgive me mama. And goodbye!

Abhi'

He looked up at the policeman who folded the letter and kept it back in the evidence bag.

Varun covered his face with his hands.

' I am not sure,' he said again after a while, trying to override the agitation inside him. The policeman touched his shoulder lightly and walked away towards the staircase. The other one followed him. Varun waited till the sound of their footsteps died away. Then he closed the door and broke into a flood of tears.

*****

Winning Wings

It was Makar Samkranti, the day the sun enters the zodiac sign of Capricorn. Every year the festival of Makar Samkranti is celebrated with much pomp and splendour in different parts of our country. The most important event that happens at some regions, is kite flying. People of all ages prepare for the kite-flying competition. The object was to cut the line of your contender's kite flying in the air. They make or buy kites and *firkee* s which are wooden spools with handles. They roll the thread which was covered with glue and ground glass onto the reel. This was done to give a sharpness to the line for cutting the thread of others' kites. Kites of several shapes and sizes and colour throng the sky on this day.

Shubbu was very busy on that Makar Samkranti. His father had given him money to buy kites and thread. He wanted to process the thread with powdered glass and glue like his elder brother did. But father strongly refused it. 'Boys of your age do not use processed thread for kite-flying,' he had warned. Shubbu had bought two kites, colourful and attractive ones. He just wanted to fix a tail to each to make it look more attractive while they drift about in the distant sky. The curls and twists the tails form while flying make them look like swimming snakes. Only that they swim in the sky.

++ ++   ++   ++

Shubbu and his brother Bubu were on the roof of Shubbu's house. Bubu was an expert kite flyer. Shubbu, only eleven, had not yet mastered the skill of kite-flying. But once he got the kite launched, he could manage well. Bubu, five years older than him, could cut the kite of others expertly. He would get his opponent's kite entangled in his line and give a sharp tug to the line by a skilful rolling of the handles of his spool or *firkee* . The thread of the opponent's kite would snap in mid-air and the kite would come hurtling down.

Shubbu rolled the handles of the spool and Bubu holding the side edges of the kite gave it a upward push. The kite fluttered for a few seconds then caught the wind and began soaring up. Shubbu, changing his position from time to time and pulling at the string sometimes by hand and by rolling of the spool made it steadily rise up. Father pushed Bubu's kite up and then Bubu made the kite take a steady upward rise expertly as he always did. Their father stood watching.

'Look Shubbu,' Bubu shouted in joy, 'my kite has reached up to the sky. It is looking so small from here. Your kite is just floating aimlessly much below mine.' Shubbu felt bad. 'Brother's kite is flying so nicely because father had helped him to launch it,' he thought enviously. 'Why didn't father push my kite up?' He tried to handle the spool with a little more force to make the kite go up higher. But it could not reach up to the height of Bubu's kite. Disappointed, Shubbu pulled at the string of his kite. It looked lovely, like a pink, diamond shaped bird with a twisting, green ribbon like strip of a tail.

His unblinking gaze followed the pink kite up into

the sky. Suddenly from nowhere another kite appeared close to Shubbu's. It was a black and silver striped one and its tail was silvery and long. Shubbu struggled desperately with his spool, rolling and twisting its handles to pull the line of his kite away from the silver-black one. But the wind did not seem to favour the movement of Shubbu's kite and it got entangled in the thread of the silver-black kite. The thread of Shubbu's kite snapped and the pink diamond shaped bird took a sharp nosedive down. Hapless and broken hearted , Shubbu watched it land on a roof adjacent to their own. '

'Hey, look at that!' Bubu cried out. 'Your kite fell......' tch!!..tch!!' he chuckled. 'Look at mine. It is flying so well.'

Father put a consoling hand on Shubbu's back. 'Don't feel so sad. You can bring it back and try again. Bubu is older than you. He can handle it with more expertise. You can also do that when you are his age.'

Shubbu ran towards the stairs. He would go to their neighbour's house, collect his kite and fly it with more care, he decided. He was about to climb down when he heard his father calling him back.

'Come back here, Shubbu,' he said looking at their neighbour's roof.

'Look.......' he pointed his finger at the kite lying on the roof. A pigeon that was waddling on the roof had somehow got its claw entwined in the string of the kite. It tried to untwine its claw from the grip of the string. Failing in its effort the bird took off to the sky spreading its wings that shone a grey and green in the afternoon sun. It soared higher and higher and the kite flew merrily in the wind. It swept past all other kites that had thronged in the sky and became a tiny pink dot.

'Saw that?' His father asked, his eyes smiling. 'I have defeated them all, father! My kite has gone up much higher than theirs!'Shubbu's voice trembled in excitement.

'You haven't won. It is the pigeon that took your kite so far into the sky!' Bubu sounded envious.

'Yes, my son,' father said affectionately.

' Nothing can stop you when destiny gives wings to your dreams.'

Bubu smiled now, happy for his brother.

Shubbu did not understand much of what his father said. He stretched his gaze high up into the sky. The tiny pink dot was no longer seen. Perhaps it had found its destination somewhere beyond the sky.

*****

Under the Palasha[1] Tree

' A story is like a moving train...no matter where you hop on board you are bound to reach the destination sooner or later. ' Someone important has said once.

This story of Vikram and Vineeta begins at the end, and here and there at some given points the scattered mid-portions could be salvaged from the depth of time, without which the story would appear discordant and sketchy.

'Where are you?'

He spoke into the screen of his phone, looking here and there for her.

'Right in front of the Administrative Block. Have you reached the P.G Council Hall?

'I am just passing that.'

'Ok. Take the left turn.'

He turned the car to the left.

He could see her now. She was there, standing by the gate in a blue silk sari, half of her face covered by the big sunglasses, her hair rolled fashionably into a knot. Vikram felt himself transformed into the young school boy he was

---

1   *Palasha A middle sized deciduous tree with brilliant orange-red flowers(Butea monosperma)*

when he had seen her first time in the class room. That was almost forty years ago. But she was still a frail and quaint figure as she always was, in the school and in the initial college days. He pulled up the car under a big leafy tree close to the spot where she stood waiting. The tree brought back the memory of the warm, summer evening long lost in Time. Vikram tried to shake the nostalgia off his mind. It seemed a futile effort, though.

Veenita looked at the slowly and uncertainly approaching vehicle. She pushed her sunglasses up her head. The person who got out of the car did not look much different from the Vikram she knew earlier, even after four decades. He was the same six feet tall, fair complexioned, handsome figure. The only change that had come over him that he had put on some weight, wore glasses and the boyish charm he exuded was replaced by a matured nuance.

She took off the sun glasses and walked over to the car. And they looked into each other's eyes after what seemed a century. Veenita tried to smile but her lips felt stiff. She just stared at him blankly basked in the warm glow inside her. Vikram did not say a word. Vineeta could see his eyes behind the glasses looked heavy with some untold sorrow. The years between them seemed to shrink and shrink to a wispy patch of smoke and evaporate into the air leaving behind only that hypnotic moment that has become an eternity.

'We should not stand here like this. Get in to the car,' Vikram said returning to his natural good humoured self, his lips curled in the mischievous smile that had never failed to charm her. Vikram was always a jovial character, a happy-go-lucky type of boy who could easily turn any serious ambience to a cheerful one.

She climbed into the passenger's seat. Vikram walked round the car and took his position behind the wheel. Vineeta remembered the one single ride with him many, many years ago. It was his uncle's fiat car, blue and glossy. Vikram could handle a car with a rare expertise even at that age. He had returned to his uncle's house after his pre-university exams were over. Her theory exams were over too. Only the practical exams were to be held a fortnight after. They used to meet outside the ladies hostel where she was staying. Sometimes they visited movies too. There was a relatively isolated spot under a big Palash tree inside the campus of the college. They used to stand under the tree and talk sweet nothings hours on end.

'How many years since we had met last?'

Vikram's voice brought her back to the present. She smiled. ' Let's not gauge time,' she said taking out a wrist watch, an expensive affair, from her vanity bag.

'Give me your hand'

Vikram took off the watch he was wearing and held it out to her. 'Here, all yours!' He said, his eyes twinkling. She tied the watch around his wrist. ' Here, I gift you my eternity, '

'Our eternity!' He said, looking deep into her eyes.

'Where would you like to go?'

'To our school,' Veenita said without thinking.

'But the school is changed. It has been extended to house a higher secondary unit. It has become a semi-college now.'

'We won't go inside. We will sit on the embankment of the river and watch it, reminiscing our school days,'

'Ok madam! At your service!' Vikram started the engine and let the car smoothly work its way out through the not-too-thick traffic of the mid-April.

'How is life with you?' Vikram asked, not taking his eyes off the road.

'So, so'!

'What sort of an answer is that? So, So!!'

'It means life has been ok with me. Not too exciting, not too dull. And yours? How is your wife? How many children?'

'My wife is very cooperative. She has been a great support. I think I could not have managed life the way I did without her support. She is so caring and so efficient! '

Vikram was effusive in praise of his wife.

' And children?'

'Am lucky on that front too. A daughter and a son. Both are married and well settled. Two adorable grandchildren as bonus. I am reasonably happy. No grievances against life.'

Surprisingly Vineeta did not feel even a grain of envy when Vikram narrated about his happy family. She felt happy and relieved. She wondered how should she have felt if Vikram was not happy in life. She would have felt guilty, or disappointed. Perhaps that is how real love is! Unselfish!! She was genuinely happy to know that Vikram had experienced the satisfaction of a fulfilled life. She smiled contentedly.

' How about your husband? What kind of a man is he? And your children and grand children? '

'Oh, he is like most husbands of the world. I have two sons. Both married and settled in life. Two grandchildren. I am also in a way satisfied and have no complaints against life,' Veenita said evasively.

' What is 'in a way' supposed to mean?'

'It means average. Not too on this side, not too on that side. Well balanced,' Veenita said through a smile.

' You are always so mysterious. I have never understood you how ever hard I tried!

'Do not try.' Veenita laughed. 'Focus on the driving.'

' You are something more than being mysterious. You are so distracting! How can I concentrate on driving sitting so close to you after ages?'

'Mind you,' Veenita pronounced a mock warning. You will get both of us killed that way.'

'Are you afraid of dying with me?'

'No. But I am sure an expert driver like you cannot get himself and his old time romantic fantasy killed through irresponsible driving.'

They reached the school. Vikram parked the car by the roadside. An early summer breeze was blowing gently. They got down and looked at the school.

'It looks so different. But the row of asbestos topped rooms on the right side where our classes were held are still the same. Aren't they?'

' Yes, they haven't demolished that section. But I think they are no longer used as the classrooms. Look, the third one from the compound wall was our class room.'

'Yes. And look at the window. You used to sit on the bench by that window, remember?'

'Of course. And you sat on the front bench on the other side and turned your head to look at me when I told my name to the teacher on my first day in the school.'

A leaf came off a balding tree that stood a little away like a dispassionate spectator, swung in the air for a few seconds and dropped on the spot like a moment in nostalgia that has wrenched itself off the vastness of time, determined to stay.

Veenita moved towards the stone bench by the embankment and sat down. Vikram stood behind her resting his palms on the backrest slab of the bench.

'The river has not changed a bit,' he said breathing a deep sigh, a distant look in his eyes.

'Yes', Veenita said in a voice so small that it could have been less than a whisper. Her thoughts travelled down into the depth of time, lower, and lower.

Vineeta's Memory Page

It was recess time. In those days there were no such thing as snacks break or lunch break. School commenced at 10.30 in the morning and the classes were over at 16.30. There was a break of one hour after the fourth period at about 13.30 or so. That time was called the recess time. Students played and went out of the main gate to buy peanuts, berries, fritters and ice cream during that break.

She heard about Vikram for the first time during one such 'recess'.

'Do you know ? A new boy has joined our class.'

It was Nima, Veenita's best friend.

'Where is he from?'

'Do not know for sure. But from some place in western Odisha. His father or uncle has been transferred to our town. '

'Is he a very good student?'

'How do I know that? I just saw him now. He is playing football with Bittu and others in the playground. A tall boy.'

Veenita was worried. She was in class eighth and had always stood first in the class. A new arrival from another town might put her position at stake. What if the boy was a better student than her? What if he stood first in the class beating Veenita? She was getting increasingly curious about the new boy.

The bell rang announcing the end of the recess hour and they all scrambled into class room amidst chatters and giggles. Their class teacher strode into the class room and the noise got subsided.

Sit down and maintain total silence. He commanded.

All sat down. 'Students! Today a new boy has joined this class. The new student will introduce himself now.

The boy who sat by the window in the last but one bench in the row to the teacher's right stood up slowly but confidently. All eyes turned in his direction. He was taller than other boys, donned in a clean white shirt and a pair of brown pants. Since it was his first day in this school, he was not wearing the school uniform.

'Tell the class about yourself, your name and other details.' The class teacher asked the boy.

'My name is Vikram Ray. I was studying in a High School at Deogarh where I stayed with my uncle. My father was posted at a different town in south Odisha . My uncle got transferred to this place and so I had to change my school.' He said in a small but steady voice.

'OK Vikram we all wish you well and welcome you to this class. By the way what is your hobby?

'I like to sing and do mimicry, sir.'

'Really? Let's first listen to a song from you and then you can do some mimicry too.'

Veenita turned again to look at the boy. He began singing, a prayer song it was. He had a captivating voice. 'He sings melodiously. Doesn't he?' Nima said nudging her. Veenita did not say a word. The song ended and the whole class applauded.

'That was really good. Now do some mimicry.'

'Whom shall I mimic, sir?'

'Any one you want to.'

'Fine sir, I will try to imitate Jatin Das, the AIR news reader.'

Then he began.... imitating the famous news reader's sonorous voice. 'Akash Vani....!! and the next minute or two were of sheer amazement.

Veenita kept staring at the boy, till long after the sound of the applause died down.

Sir was very pleased with the new boy. He went near the boy and patted his back. Vikram seemed to have a magnetic pull. He seemed to be having a joie de vivre about himself and could humour people easily. The whole class was instantly drawn towards him.

Suddenly his eyes fell on Veenita, who turned her head away feeling utterly embarrassed. The teacher had started teaching and the attention of the class shifted to him.

Veenita Gupta could not remember exactly how it all started. Perhaps it was on the very first day while Vikram flashed a secret and mischievous smile at her while they were making their way out of the main gate of the school, or on that rainy day when they were standing in two rows facing each other on the veranda of the class room and one of her friends pushed her forward making her bump into Vikram who stood in front of her, or that day after the school she was returning home alone ang looking back saw Vikram and his friend walking behind her. She looked at Vikram and he had given her a mysterious smile.

A few days later Vikram's cousin sister Shobha who was one year junior in school took her to an unfrequented spot in the large playground and gave her a picture-cutting of Lord Shiva and Parvati, looking serious as if she was giving some illegal or banned object to her.

'Brother's gift for you,' she said, her lips now curling a little in the semblance of a smile. Perhaps that was the first link in the chain of such small episodes that pulled them closer. Surprisingly they had never spoken to each other except in a few occasions like she requesting him to draw for her a sketch of a frog in the science examination half yearly test. Their names started with V and so her seat, alphabetically ordered, was just behind him and close to the rear wall of the hall. He had asked for an additional sheet to the invigilator, drawn the sketch of the frog and slipped back the sheet to her while the invigilator was looking in the other direction. There were other occasions all of which she could not recollect chronologically, but the random episodes like the Ganesh and Saraswati puja, the school annual function, teacher's day and the song and debate competitions where they had spoken a few formal words to each other. It was always the affectionate and loyal Shobha through whom they kept connected with each other. There was never an exchange of letters, never a clandestine meeting, but they as if were bonded up together by some invisible knot.

The next year she changed school. Her father insisted that she must join a better school and got her admitted one of the best girls' High Schools of the town. The memory of the day her father came to get the school leaving certificate from the office was vivid in her mind. Vikram, looking miserable stood leaning against a pillar. His eyes held the pain of some unseeable wound somewhere deep inside. But he did not say a word when all her classmates bade her farewell. The look of agony in Vikram's eyes haunted her long after she came back home. She felt restless and hardly slept for an hour or two that night.

She liked her new school and the new friends. Vikram was slowly fading out of her memory when Shobha, his cousin joined the same school. Shobha brought Vikram back to her mind.

'Vicky bhai always remembers you. He is never tired of speaking about you,' Shobha told her when both of them were alone in the long corridor.

Veenita felt a stabbing pain at heart. 'I too miss him' The words escaped her before she could fight them off her tongue.

She took out the picture cutting she had carefully preserved between two pages in her algebra book and gave it to Shobha the next day.

'Give it to him. He will know'.

A couple of days later Shobha brought her a letter from Vikram. It was a long letter, of three or four pages where he has poured out his feelings without reserve. It was difficult for Veenita to resist the overpowering urge to see him, to speak to him but it was not possible. A few drops of helpless tears that fell on the letter smudged some words.

But she did not write a reply. She would send him a coloured plume of a bird or a picture-cutting. That was the only means through which she tried to remain connected with Vikram. Vikram too did not send any more letter. Now and then he too, would send a picture cutting or a few coloured plumes through Shobha, who acted as a loyal go-between and Veenita preserved them as priceless tokens.

Two more years passed. They had never met or spoken to each other in those two years.

The school finals drew close and Veenita got busy in studies. The thoughts of Vikram kept nagging at the back of her mind but she tried to push them away. The examinations were over. There was no scope to meet Shobha. Slowly her mind drifted away from Vikram as she got preoccupied with the future plans, the worries about the results and the chances of getting a seat in a reputed college.

Her result was out. Her father was overjoyed to learn that she had secured a first division. Incidents that followed one another kept her so occupied that she could not find much time to think of Vikram. He too did not seem to have made much effort to revive the contact, obviously for lack of appropriate communication measures. She got admission in the science stream in one of the best colleges. The pressure of studies and the stress crowded her mind too heavily to allow Vikram an entry there. Her parents went to stay in the village for some time since there was a dispute over the landed properties there between her father and uncles. Veenita had to live with her cousin brother and sister- in- law. But the distractions in their house made impossible to concentrate in studies. Her father put her in the college ladies' hostel. Hostel life suited her and she was happy to be amongst friends.

The final examination was drawing near. After filling up the form she came to her village to prepare for the examination.

It was an early summer afternoon. Father was helping her in solving the problems of mathematics. She sat amidst the scattered books and copies. The pages of book fluttered at the touch of a gentle breeze. Suddenly her eyes caught sight of something handwritten on one of the pages. She lifted the book and looked closely at it. It was an old book of trigonometry and she had not much use of it now. God only knew how it came to find a place amongst the college books.

Curious, she opened it at the page where she had seen the handwritten matter.

It was a postal address and was not in her handwriting. She tried to recollect and it suddenly came back to her who has written it and whose address was it. Long back in her final year at school Shobha has written it. 'Brother will go back to Deogarh after the school finals. He can be reached at this address. You can write to this address if you like,'

It has gone completely out of Veenita's mind. Now, after almost two years she discovered the address by a stroke of sheer chance. Her mind refused to register what her father was saying. The memory of Vikram, the gloomy look in his eyes on the day when she last saw him leaning against the pillar, came rushing back to her. She felt lost and breathless, submerged under the huge tides of some unspeakable emotion.

That evening she wrote a letter to Vikram, her first letter in almost five years. It was not very personal though. She had inquired about his studies, his health and whereabouts. She was not sure whether the letter would ever reach him. Next day she went to the village post office alone and dropped it in the post box, with the least hope of a reply.

A week passed. The final examination was a few days away. She was preparing to return to the college hostel. The reply came a day before she was to leave her village.

She hopped up the flight of stairs, taking two steps at a time, to the rooftop. Her breath was coming in loud gasps as she sat down in a corner and opened the envelope. Though the sun has set, there was enough light for reading the letter.

It was a long letter written in a neat hand. Vikram has vented out all his pent-up emotions, all his longings he had buried in his heart for the last five years in the pages of the letter. He said that he would come to meet her in her college hostel on the seventh of May, immediately after her theory papers were over. His examinations would have been over by that time too, he said.

Veenita's heart leaped in joy. There would be no bounds, no rigid regulations in meeting Vikram now. She waited desperately for the examination to be over.

Vikram's Memory Page

The first person his eyes fell on as he entered the class room was her. She sat in the front bench a quaint, dainty, charming thing.

The crowd of students was jostling its way into the class room, and he did not get much chance to take a good look at her. Then sir asked him to do some mimicking and sing a song. He was feeling ill at ease in the new school and the new environment. But he had made some friends during the recess hour and had played football with them. He stood up, feeling nervous. All eyes were turned towards him. The girl from the front bench too turned to look at him. Now he had a full view of her face, her aquiline nose, big, black eyes, thick curved brows, and her glistening full lips.

Saying a silent prayer he stood up and began to sing. It was a prayer song. Then he mimicked a famous AIR newsreader. The teacher and the class looked visibly impressed. The teacher came to him and gave him an affectionate pat on the back. The boys looked at him with admiration. He was no longer nervous.

The girl in the front bench was still looking back. For a moment their eyes met, and she turned her face away. The final bell rang and they moved out of the class. The girls walked behind, gossiping and giggling. Subrat put a hand on his shoulder,

' You are too good buddy!'

'It's no big deal,' Vikram laughed. Soon others joined and they began making plans for tomorrow's football game. They had reached the main gate of the school. He looked back. The girl was just behind him. He flashed a naughty smile at her. The girl looked down, increased her pace and leaving the other girls behind she ran past the boys and went out of the gate.

'Hey, Vini', a girl called out. Why are you in such a hurry today?'

'She must be very hungry,' another girl said and they all laughed. Vikram's gaze followed the girl whose name was Vini, hoping that she would cast a glance behind. But she didn't.

Then there was that rainy day. The students were standing in two rows facing each other on the veranda. He was standing close to a pillar. Vini had not yet reached. The prayer was about to start. She came running and stood beside her close friend Nima who stood just on front of him. Vini was breathless from running hard. Suddenly the girl called Saroja, who had squeezed herself between Vini and another girl gave Vini a push. Vini pitched forward and bumped into him. He, to save himself from falling pressed his hand to the pillar exerting a great force. They both would have fallen off the veranda otherwise. Vini, embarrassed, and glum, took her position next to Nima. The boys and girls laughed. But the teacher arrived at that moment and everyone became silent. He looked secretly at Vini while singing the refrain of the prayer song. She looked visibly embarrassed and her eyes were heavy with a wetness. He felt sad.

Days rolled on. He spoke to Vini on few occasions and she also replied. But all the while the conversation was formal. He was feeling so drawn to Vini that he began to feel restless if she was even five minutes late for the school. He found out her house with the help of Subrat, who had now become his close friend and confidante.

He was desperate to talk to her, to feel her presence from close quarters. Then it struck his mind like a lightning flash.

Shobha! His cousin sister!!

Shobha was one year junior to them in the same school. She was close to Vikram too. It took five rupees and some cajoling to persuade Shobha to act as a go-between. He sent a few picture- cuttings to Veenita to begin with. Nothing happened for a week. On the day before the Puja holidays were due to start Shobha brought him a plume. A tiny soft and pink coloured plumes..... a return gift from Vini. That day she turned to glance at him and her lips curved in a lovely smile. Vikram's heart swelled, his imagination soared high and drifted along with the white autumn clouds to some wonderland beyond the sky.

He got a bit closer to her during the half yearly test. Her seat was just behind him in the examination hall. It was the day of the science test. The invigilator was making his regular pacing along the aisles between the rows of seats. He heard Vini calling him in a subdued voice. 'Yes', he whispered back without glancing back. 'Could you please draw the sketch of a frog for me?' She whispered.

'Sure,' he said and stood up. 'Additional paper, sir,' he said.

The invigilator returned carrying a bunch of

additional papers and handed one to Vikram. He sat down and drew the sketch of a frog on it. After completing he sneaked it behind to Vini avoiding the eyes of the invigilating teacher.

Vini came to him after the final bell rang and thanked him 'Sorry about troubling you,' she said blushing a little. 'No problem at all,' he said. Vini walked away. 'Vini,' he called her without thinking. She stopped, turned and looked at him, question in her dark eyes. Vikram did not know what to say though he was bursting with emotions.

'It's nothing. Sorry.' He gave an embarrassed smile. Vini flicked a knowing smile at him. Her friend Nima arrived and they both went away.

He did not remember speaking intimately to Vini on any occasion during the school days. The communication, very little though, was made only through Shobha. But he was happy and contented with that.

But the happiness did not last long. Vini changed school next year. She took transfer certificate from the old school and joined another. He would never forget the pain and agony of the day Vini left the school. He stood outside the sports room, leaning against a pillar watching her walking out of the office of the Head Master with her father. The boys and the girls of their class were bidding her farewell and wishing her luck. His eyes fell on Nima. Her eyes were red from weeping. She and Vini were very close after all. Were he a girl like Nima he also could have wept, Vikram thought bitterly. But he did not go near Vini to bid her fare well or wish luck.

Why should she have to leave this school, after all? He wanted to say so many things to her but could never speak more than a sentence or two. He walked away from the place silently, feeling broken hearted.

School was like a desert after Vini went away. He wanted badly to see her, just to have a small glimpse of her.

On many occasions he walked past the street in front of her house hoping desperately for the front door to open and Vinni appear at it. But the door never opened. He became friendly with a boy who lived in the neighbourhood of Vini. The name of the boy was Kishore and he studied in the same class Vikram did, but in another school. Kishore had taken an instant liking to Vikram and soon they both began to spend time in each other's house. Subrat also joined them in most occasions. But Vikram and Subrat did not tell him anything about Vini. Sometimes as they sat on the roof of Kishore's house Vikram caught a brief glimpse of Vini. But that was all. He never got a chance to meet or speak to her.

Then Shobha joined the school where Vini studied. Vikram was happy. He could be in touch with Vini through Shobha. While he was in two minds whether to write a letter to her or not since he was not sure if she was interested in him, Shobha brought him something unexpectedly. It was the first picture-cutting he had given to Vini. He was puzzled. Why had Vini returned it? Why had she preserved it for so many days if she intended to give it back? Or, Vikram thought hopefully, she wanted him to say something? He decided to take a chance and wrote a long letter venting out all his untold feelings for her in it. He waited for a week. No reply from Vini came. Another week passed. He stopped hoping for a reply. He guessed that Vini was feeling shy or embarrassed to write back to him. Occasionally she sent a coloured plume of a bird or picture-cutting through Shobha. That was the only way they communicated with each other.

But it did not last long. The school finals were over and it was almost impossible to keep in touch with Vini.

He left for Deogarh to pursue higher studies and all contact with Vini was snapped. He had requested Shobha to meet Vini for once and give her the postal address of Deogarh in case she wanted to communicate. In the summer vacation following the first-year examination of the two year course of the Intermediate Arts he had come to Vini's town. Shobha, was now in the final year of the school.

'Did you give the address to her?'

Vikram asked Shobha when they were alone.

'Yes, bhai. I had met her in the market only a few days ago. She has got a first division and is now studying Intermediate Science in the best college of our town. She was with her mother. We couldn't talk much but I have told her to contact you on that address.'

'Did you give her it in writing?'

'Yes bhai. I wrote it down on a page of an old trigonometry book I was carrying. She had put it in her satchel bag which she was carrying for shopping.'

'I think she has misplaced the book and forgotten about it, ' Vikram let out a deep sigh.

'Don't you worry bhai,' Shobha said consolingly. ' I will try to go to her home or send it to her through someone reliable.'

But Shobha got seriously engaged in preparing for the ensuing final examination. The promise she had made to her brother was forgotten in the preoccupation and the anxiety.

And then, after one more year, when he was expecting it the least, the long awaited letter from Vini came. The letter was brief but intense. She would be staying in the hostel for more than a month after her theory examinations, she said and asked if he could come to meet her there. He was excited enough to bring the roof down.

Vikram wrote a long reply that very night and assured that he would.

That Summer

It was an unforgettable summer for Vikram and Veenita. The memory of that month of exuberance and ecstasy remained forever afresh in their minds.

'Veenita Gupta, ' the lady peon of the hostel announced, 'visitor for you.'

Vini had stopped waiting for Vikram. He was supposed to arrive on the 7th. But he did not. He did not come the next day, nor the day after. A whole week passed. Vinni lost all hope. 'Why should he come this far to meet me?' She asked herself, trying to reason out. 'School days are over and so also the childlike sentiment of the school days. He might have transferred his interest to someone else.'

But a thought persistently nagged at her mind. 'Why did he reply her letter, then? Why made the promise?'

She was not sure what was in Vikram's mind, but she had somehow got over the restlessness of waiting for him.

'Visitor for you, Veenita Gupta,' the peon announced again. She picked up the stole from the bedpost and walked towards the visitors' hall of the hostel and there he was, standing on the porch, looking more handsome now in a turquoise green full-sleeved shirt tucked neatly into a pair of black trousers. She stopped abruptly, and they just stood there looking at each other, unblinking, rooted. At that never ending moment of ecstasy the earth stopped coursing its orbit, the sky froze. She had heardit happens in romantic songs only but never believed it could really happen. A minute passed and Vikram broke the silence.

'Hey! Have you seen a ghost?' And smiled broadly. His eyes glowed with a mischievous sparkle, exactly the same magnetic smile that had pulled her to him years ago.

' She got hold of her emotions and smiled back. 'Why didn't you come on the 7th? I was waiting so desperately! I thought you 'd never come.'

' Will that be ever possible? You would wait for me and I wouldn't come!'

Then followed the series of long chatting. They walked to the column of gulmohar and palash trees and stood under them talking and talking endlessly. He left when it was lunch time and came back soon. The sun blazed, but they did not feel it. The day ended and the moon came up. 'You must leave now. I cannot stay out of the hostel after evening without the prior permission of the superintendent.

'But I don't want to go away from you,' he made a gloomy face. Veenita laughed. ' 'Come back early tomorrow, 'she said. ' I can't wait for the night to end,' he said in his natural drawling voice and left.

The days of summer flew away like winged things. Every morning by nine Vikram would reach the hostel and they would stand talking sweet nothings till it was lunchtime and he would come back in the afternoon. Her practical examinations started but she was not very serious about it. Her world was now full of Vikram. But Vikram, very discreetly did not come on the days of her examination. He discharged other duties assigned to him by his family during those days.

They went to movies, walking all the way, talking and talking nonstop. Neither of them actually watched the movies. They just sat together holding hands for the two and half hours. And then the time came for Veenita to go back to her village. Her examinations were over. There was no other excuse for her to continue her staying in the hostel.

The evening before her father was due to take her back to village, they went to see a movie. It was getting close to nine in the evening by the time they returned. For the first time they had sat together in a rickshaw. Vikram asked the rickshaw puller to stop by a lassi stall and brought two large glasses of lassi. He spread his hankie on Vineeta's lap. 'How thoughtful of you!' Veenita teased. 'You are my most precious thing. I must be thoughtful when it comes to you!' He said feelingly.

The rickshaw was moving slowly. It reached the Palash tree under which they used to stand for hours talking. Moonlight filtered through the leaves, and a soft warm breeze blew. Vikram put her left arm around Veenita and pulled her closer and kissed her. It was just a tender and shy brushing of lips on her cheek. Veenita closed her eyes and snuggled into his embrace. He kissed her again, and then again.

The rickshaw moved out of the enigmatic shade of the rows of trees and Vikram released her. 'Don't forget me,' he said his voice breaking a little. 'I won't. 'Write to me!' Veenita whispered, tears in her eyes. They reached the hostel gate and Veenita climbed down. Vikram held her hand in a tight grip for a while and then freed it. 'Bye!' he said.

'Bye!' Veenita waved her hand and ran into the hostel, her heart bursting with unreleased sobs.

The days that followed the goodbye were days of unbearable agony. And waiting....

waiting for the letters. It took about a week for a letter from Deogarh to reach her village. Veenita lived each week in waiting. She had a little cousin brother who when bribed with chocolates and money, dropped her letters in the post box. Time rolled on. Her results came. She got a second division. Father was visibly disappointed. Vikram too got a second division and had decided to go ahead with Economics as an honours subject. She was yet to decide if she would continue in the science stream or change to humanities. After much deliberation it was finally decided that she would switch to the humanities. She was getting ready for returning to the town and seek a fresh admission into the arts stream.

And then the disaster struck.

That day she had waited for Vikram's letter till two in the afternoon. The post man usually came around 12.30 or 1.00 pm. Assuming that the letter wouldn't come that day she went with her cousins and friends to the mango grove, their favourite hangout.

She returned home after five. Her father was sitting

by the front door waiting for her. There was something in her father's face which frightened her. He did not look his usual gentle self. To Veenita, he looked like a stranger.

He waved an envelope at her. 'What is this? What have you been doing in the hostel?

Father shouted, fuming. Veenita stood rooted, her heart at her throat. She tried to speak, but what escaped her mouth was an unintelligible mumble. She knew that her feeble explanation would not help her a bit. She kept standing holding her head down.

'Now I know why you could not get a first class. Your mind was not in the studies! You will not stay in the hostel any more. For the time being I will make arrangements for you to stay with the family of one of my friends. We will be moving to the town very soon. As such I have not much work here now.'

Helpless tears streamed down her eyes.

' Light the evening lamp for the evening worship, ' mother said and signalled her to leave the place. She thanked mother silently and went to the puja room, dragging her feet which seemed to have grown heavy suddenly.

The incidents that followed it made her drift away from Vikram. She had got a letter posted to Vikram through her cousin brother asking him not to write to her anymore. Time had taken a cruel turn.

She stayed in the house of her father's friend for a few days and then her parents moved to the town. Her elder brother had got a transfer to the same town in the meantime and he stayed with them. Father had entrusted her brother to keep a close watch on Vini.

There was almost nil chance to meet Vikram or even communicate with him. Shobha was now pursuing higher studies in a college in another town. About six or so months after Vikram had come to her town. He had sent words through Subrat who met her for a few minutes in the college to intimate her. He had written a very short letter asking her to wait for him outside the gate of the college.

Vini stood a little away from the college gate that afternoon and waited eagerly for Vikram. A minute later she saw him approaching. He looked pale and lean. Vini wanted badly to touch his face, to tell him how she suffered.

'Can we go to some place where we can have some privacy?' Vikram asked.

'Let's walk to that palash tree at the far end of the campus road we used to stand under. We can talk while walking'

They began walking, careful to maintain a reasonable distance to avoid suspicion.

They reached the palash tree. There was no one around.

Vikram held Vini's hand in a tight grip.

'I cannot live without you!' His voice was hoarse with emotion.

Vini touched his hand. Tears rolled down her eyes. Her lips trembled but she could not say a word.

She saw a group of boys coming towards the tree riding bicycles. Vini took her hand off Vikram's grip.

'Let's go now. More students will come. The final period is over. We will meet here tomorrow. Try to come a little early.'

'Yes,' Vikram agreed and they walked back towards the main gate. A young man was sitting astride a bicycle by the gate. Vini's heart began to beat wildly. It was her brother. 'Go away soon. My brother is there at the gate.' Without waiting for Vikram's reply she ran to the gate, gasping for breath.

'Your classes were over half an hour back. What were you doing in the college? ' He demanded. 'I was in the library,' Vini stammered. 'I will go inside to fetch you if you are late again. Library, my foot!' Don't do anything you shall regret later,' he threatened.

Viinita sat on the rear seat of the bicycle, greatly relieved that her brother had not seen Vikram.

+ + +   + + +   + + +   + + +

Vikram looked again at his watch. It was going to be four thirty. Most of the classes were over. Students were walking down the road in groups and solo. He had been standing under the familiar palash tree, their favourite meeting spot for nearly forty five minutes waiting for Vini, but there was no sign of her. He had been doing this for the last two days but Vini never came.

He was now filled with premonitions. 'Has something happened to Vini? Has her father somehow found out that they had met?' He stretched his gaze to the far end of the road. No. No sign of Vini. 'Is she trying to avoid me?' He was not sure but he could not fight the feeling back. He breathed a deep sigh and walked away from the place.

Vini touched her ankle gingerly and winced. It was aching and badly swollen. Last night there was a power failure and she had twisted her ankle while she was coming out of her room to light a candle. What seemed a small accident now has turned out to be a very painful experience. She was not able to walk. She lay helplessly on the bed and thought about Vikram. He must have waited for her. What would he have thought? He must have been disappointed and also angry with her. There was no way to let him know of her miserable plight.

She felt a little better a couple of days after. Despite the doctor's cautioning she went to the college hoping against hope that Vikram would be there under the palash tree waiting for her. She stood under the tree for a long time but Vikram did not come. The next day she again went to the spot but he was not there. A week passed. Vikram did not return.

Then Subrat came to the college looking for her.

'What happened? Where is Vikram?' Vini asked eagerly. She told him why she could not come to meet Vikram that day.

'I am sorry to know about your accident. Vikram left for Deogarh that very night. He did not even meet me before leaving.'

Vini did not say anything.

' I will let you know if he writes to me.' Subrat left.

'He should have waited at least for a few days to know why I couldn't come. Let him be happy there. I wouldn't disturb him again.' She decided and limped back to the gate where her brother was waiting.

They never met again.

They yearned for each other, were torn with untold longings but there was something that held them back. What followed is simple and short. Vini did her postgraduation and got married to the boy chosen by her parents and settled at another town. She got appointed as a lecturer in a college. Vikram too got a job as a marketing manager in an insurance company and he also got married to a girl of his father's choice.

All contact between them was cut off. But a sense of loss, though not very pronounced, haunted them in their solitary hours.

It was after four decades, when she had come back to the town where she had lived and studied, Vinita met someone in a family gathering who by sheer chance mentioned Vikram. Vinita stretched the conversation with the lady and discovered that she was a distant cousin of Vikram. She collected the contact number of Vikram from her.

Suddenly, the memory lying dormant for so many years sprang back to life. She did not know it at that time but the lady who introduced herself as Vikram's cousin had called Vikram and told him about their meeting.

Vikram picked up the phone at the first ring. 'I have been waiting for your call since yesterday. How are you?'

Vini gripped the phone with all her strength as if she held Vikram's hand. Her palms were clammy and sweat trickled down from behind her ears. She fumbled for words and then, her voice quivering with overwhelming emotions she muttered,

'I am fine. I thought you have forgotten me!'

'You are silly even now as you were then.' He laughed, the same mischievous laughter. ' I want to meet you. When and where can we meet? '

' I will let you know. Give me a little time.'

'Why do you need 'a little time'? If I die in that 'little time', I cannot see you and my ghost will haunt you day and night.'

'Look who is being silly now. You have been haunting me all these years like a ghost. Do not worry. Neither I nor you are going to die without seeing each other. We will meet day after tomorrow. I will text you the time and place.'

I can't wait to see you. Just do not keep me waiting under the palash tree,' he laughed.

Vini felt a sharp prick at her heart.

'Okay, bye.' She said and broke the connection.

++   ++   ++   ++   ++

A truck juddered past. The shrill blare jerked Vini out of her reverie. She smiled apologetically. ' Sorry I was lost in our past.'

'' I too. Had it not been for that loud sound of the horn I would have been still floundering my way out of it, though to be honest, I want to remain lost, forever!,' he sighed.

'What is the point? ' Vini said sadly. ' This is like as if we stand leaning against a wall of mist! Who knows had we been a little patient and a little brave we would have never been separated.'

'It is much better this way. There is no expectation, no anxiety, no apprehension ....' He touched Vini's hand.

'Maybe you are right!' She said and rose to her feet. Vikram stood up too.

' Shall we go to the tree where we used to meet?' He looked into the eyes of Veenita.

'I was about to suggest that,' she lowered her eyes. Even at that age Vikram's intense look embarrassed her.

They drove down the long road that glinted a brilliant black in the mid -April sunshine.

'I had always dreamt of this kind of a ride, I mean sitting beside you , going on a long drive in a lonely road,' Vini said smiling contentedly. ' It took more than forty years to be realized.' She added.

'But I would have preferred sitting together in a train face to face where I can have a full view of you. Here I have to keep my eyes glued to the road.'

'There is nothing in me for you to appraise now. I have grown old.'

'Really? To me you are always the girl in a blue frock sitting on the front bench. And, he turned his face to look at her deeply, ' the young woman in the green sari who sat beside me in the cycle rickshaw that warm evening of May .... my first love ...under the palash tree.'

It was too late when he saw the onrushing truck. He struggled desperately with the steering wheel to get through a sideway. The car swerved violently and hit the long culvert on the roadside with tremendous force and upturned. Something white hot exploded inside his head. The last sound he heard before darkness descended on him was the wild scream of Vini. Then there was total silence.

A big, moon shone in the April sky. The moonlight filtered through the big palash tree and formed mysterious patterns below. A nightbird hooted somewhere in another tree. Two shadows moving gently on the mass of the dark red petals of palash lying under the tree advanced towards each other.

They stood still facing each other for a fractured moment, then merged into each other and became one.

A thin patch of cloud swept over the moon.

*****

Shadow Circle

She sat looking into the large pool, by the bamboo clumps that swung in the light breeze blowing from the north. Under the cloudless sky of late autumn, the pool sparkled like a liquid mirror. It captured the full moon with all its glory. From the jungle beyond that was wrapped in the mist of an enigmatic green and black, the scent of exotic flowers swept over the water. The scent, like an intoxicant, made her feel a little dizzy. Somewhere, far, far away someone played a mysterious note on a flute and the leaves rustled to its tune. She closed her eyes. Someone touched her shoulder lightly. It was so light that at first, she thought that the tip of a swinging bamboo leaf from a stooping clump brushed across her shoulder. Her eyes snapped open and she jerked back. A pair of strong palms closed over her eyes and she could feel the warmth of someone's breath on her neck. 'Don't open your eyes.' A voice said gently. 'I will show you a magic', it said again. She sat still, more curious than frightened. There was something soothing in the voice that subdued her fear. Obediently she kept her eyes closed. Then she felt the touch again, on her face, on those areas where the dark patches were, on her cheeks and forehead. She tried to imagine the object the patches were being touched with. 'Must be a peacock plume,' she guessed. 'Now open your eyes and look into the water,' the voice said. Curious, she shifted along the step towards the edge of the pool and bent to look in. The calm, moonlit water caught her face flawlessly. Her face that looked bright and spotless flashed on the pool, next to that of the moon. It looked shiny and spotless, like a twin of the moon, only without its spots. Was it her face? It resembled hers in a way, and there was no one else close by to have a reflection of his or her face in the water. How could be it her face? Where were the patches, the couple of dull purple patches under her eyes and the one on her forehead? She jerked behind to find the stranger who touched her face with a feather of a bird or some such thing. There was no one there by the pool. The temple by the pool looked desolate and abandoned in that mysterious light. Not a soul was in sight. Who spoke to her? She looked again into the pool. Her face flashed in, bright and beautiful. Suddenly the wind began to blow strongly. The water in the pool stirred. Even as she looked at the reflection of the moon, it became a big black blob and went into the water. She saw her own face stirring wildly in the water and the scene changed all of a sudden.

The pool vanished and the jungles and bamboo clumps too. She was now in an empty room looking at a black and grey wall that faced her. A girl's face, it resembled her own in many ways except for the livid patches under the eyes and the forehead, appeared on it. The face was circled by a white halo. A sharp nose, big black eyes, arched eyebrows and the small full mouth looked more pronounced when seen in contrast with the black-grey wall. She squinted at the wall, to find out if the face was actually hers. Slowly, she began moving towards the wall. Just as she took a few steps towards it the wall seemed to move back, as if an invisible hand was pulling it away from her. The more steps she took towards it, the wall slid more back into the darkness behind. She stopped and the wall stopped too. Then she felt the familiar touch of a feather stroking her face tenderly. She closed her eyes. Then something strange happened which made her heart pound erratically. She opened her eyes and discovered herself standing very close to the wall, so close that the face on the wall looked blurred and hazy. It no longer looked beautiful because there were livid purple patches all over it. Suddenly the wall moved back with a great speed, and then was flooded in a blinding light. She stood staring at the light-washed wall that had gone back to some fifty meters or so. Then something happened that took her breath away. The wall came rushing at her and crumbled making an earsplitting noise. Scraps of plaster and pieces of brick flung wildly around her. She was buried under debris in the next instant. A shrill scream escaped her.

She did not remember exactly when she began hallucinating. Perhaps since the day she had overheard her parents discussing her. 'It will not be easy to find a groom for her,' father was saying. 'You know I have consulted many dermatologists. We have tried the traditional herbal treatment too. Nothing seems to work. They say that birthmarks do not go away easily.' There was a hopelessness in father's voice.

'We cannot pick up just anyone walking down the road to give our child away in marriage because she has those patches. It is better if she is educated enough to get a job and live an independent life.' Mothe remarked.

'That is right. We will need a considerate and accommodative boy who does not put physical beauty above inner goodness. There are not many young men with such kind of temperament. But imagine, who will she turn to at a matured age, when we will not be around ? whom shall she share her thoughts with? Who will give her company?' father's voice was gloomy and contrite.

'Let's leave everything in the hands of God. God must be having some plans for her.'

'God had already planned her future while He gave her those ugly birthmarks,' father heaved out a deep sigh.' He sounded lost and desperate.

Reba felt a prick at her heart. She felt sagged under the load of her parents' the desperateness. She knew the marriage proposals were getting rejected because of her looks. But for the cursed patches on her face, she was not bad to look at. Her complexion was fair and her features were sharp and well defined in her oval face. But who would want to marry a girl with those sinister looking birth marks? There were times when she seriously contemplated suicide, but her better judgment desisted her from taking such a rash step. Putting an end to her life would not be a sensible solution, nor would it bring any relief to her parents, she reasoned with herself. But the desire to get rid of the patches became an obsession. She tried all possible remedies, suggested by friends to remove the marks. She tried expensive creams that claimed to clear the skin in a week, used herbal products, and even took vitamins and minerals with a hope that they would help in making the patches a bit light if not remove them completely. No therapy seemed to work. The futile efforts and the frustration resulting out of the failures turned her into an introvert. She was unwilling to go out with her friends, as such she had only a few friends. She went routinely to college in the morning and got back home as soon as the classes were over. She sat by the window that overlooked the garden and the street beyond it, brooding. There was a rose bush in one corner of the garden. Her mother said it would grow white roses. But there never bloomed a white rose on the plant. Her eyes were instinctively dragged towards the bush, whenever she sat by the window. The rose bush stood thick and bare and lonely, in that desolate corner day after day, season after season. The marriage proposals her parents pursued kept on getting rejected, month after month, year after year.

Her marriage to Rohit was a marvelous break of luck.

It was a fine morning in early summer when her father announced the news that a young man who worked in a government office was coming to see her. Her mother received the news rather dispassionately. The continuous denials had killed her hopes. Reba wanted to tell her father not to make her go through the belittling charade of offering the candidate and his parents or relatives tea and snacks wearing a fake smile and later, swallowing the insult of their disapproval. But her father sounded hopeful and she did not have the heart to refuse him. 'Get yourself ready. They will be arriving in an hour.'

Without saying a word she went to her room and sat by the window, her heart heavy with the thought of the inevitable rejection. Her gaze wandered to the corner of the garden, to the rose bush. Something strange caught her eyes. Strange it was, indeed. On one of the top twigs of the rose plant there was a bud. She rubbed her eyes and looked intently. Yes, it was a bud. She ran out to the garden and went to the corner to examine it closely. There were a few more buds. The rose bush that had stood bare all these days had begun to grow buds. It was no less than a miracle!

It was also a miracle that neither Rohit, nor his parents rejected her. 'A person is not to be judged by her outward looks.' His mother had remarked. Rohit and his father smiled their consent. Tears of relief rolled down her father's eyes. It was a never to be forgotten moment.

The marriage was solemnized a few months later. Rohit was an indulging husband. He never mentioned the patches on her face. He rather seemed to be eager to please Reba in any manner he could. If at all Reba would make a passing remark about how grateful she was to him, Rohit would, as if he was determined not to let her say that, brush the subject aside. Reba guessed that expressing her gratefulness might embarrass her husband. She too would make an effort not to broach the subject. Life had changed. The thick fog of gloom that loomed over her mind had begun to dissipate. She had begun to believe that like those 'happily married' couples she had heard about from her friends, she also was happily married.

She had had the hallucination the day after her wedding night. It was a different version of the earlier ones. This time there was the calm water of the pond, the reflection of the big moon in it , and the soft notes of the flute floating in from afar figured in her vision. She felt the gentle touch of a feather or something like that on her face, as if someone was standing behind, very close and touching the feather on her cheeks and forehead. She could feel the warmth of someone's breath on her shoulder. But unlike the other days the touch was not accompanied with the soothing voice. Even in that state of half wakefulness she was consumed with curiosity and swung back to see who was behind.

It was Rohit! Her husband!!

'What are you brooding over so deeply?' Rohit asked, his curious gaze sweeping over her. He was back from the office.

The spell broke. She found herself sitting on the bed. The sun of the autumn afternoon slanted lazily on the wall facing the bed.

'Nothing in particular,' she answered evasively and went to the kitchen to make tea and snacks.

Strangely she had had no more visions after that day.

She had stopped hallucinating!

The distorted moon in the pool, the ugly face on the wall that had burst into a blinding white light and rushed at her, had become distant things. She drifted into a dreamless sleep listening to the gentle snoring of her husband. Her nights now broke into fresh, bright mornings.

And then Rima came to her life, to make it more beautiful. Proving all her fear and premonitions that her child might take after her mother baseless, the baby girl was flawlessly beautiful, with her mother's fair complexion and her chiseled features. She was a tiny miracle that made her life complete. She had now no complaints against her destiny, nor did she despise the patches on her face any longer. Rohit and Rima gave her a twenty four hour engagement that left her no scope to think about anything else except her little family. Time flew away on happy wings.

And then things began to change. The change came slowly, so slowly that she continued not to notice it even much after it had actually infiltrated her fulfilled world.

The small incidents, the passing remarks, the indifference coated in the decent yet formal manners were the first signs of it. But she ignored them, believing them to be just ordinary happenings.

The curtain of self-deception lifted on the evening Rohit brought the makeup kit while returning from office. They had been to a wedding anniversary party of one of Rohit's colleagues last evening, and it was late when they got home. The babysitter had put Rima, who was now three years old, to sleep. They went to bed and Reba had fallen asleep immediately.

Rohit had an official meeting to attend to and he left early the next morning. He returned late in the night. Reba served dinner for both of them on the dining table. Rohit came out from the washroom and sat down to eat. 'I have brought something for you,' he said not lifting his eyes from the plate. Reba looked up at him. 'You have always been spending money on buying things for me,' she said, her voice steeped in love. 'it's nothing like that. I have brought some imported medicated creams for you. They will help the patches on your face to fade.' Her hand carrying the food to her mouth stopped abruptly in the act. She saw Rohit munching, his eyes fixed on the plate.

'Why are you suddenly concerned about the patches? You have never even mentioned them in all these years.'

'One of my colleagues had returned from the States the day before. I had asked him to get me some medicated creams that will work effectively on the patches. What is so odd about it? Try them. It is well and good if they work. We have nothing to lose, if they don't. Isn't it?' He said without looking into her eyes.

'Yes', Reba said, struggling with her emotions. Her head was beginning to ache. She tried to eat but she found she could not swallow the food. Rohit had finished dinner. He rose to his feet. 'Give them a try.' He patted Reba's back and walked to the wash basin.

She sat awake for a long time after Rohit went to sleep. Little Rima slept soundly by him. The room was partly lit by moonlight. The moon of the fourteenth day of the bright lunar fortnight shone in the cloudless sky. She wandered to the window and looked up at the sky. The moon seemed unusually big and very close to the window. She rubbed her eyes and looked again. A cloud swept over the moon just at that moment and the room became dark. The cloud went past the moon. Reba stared at the moon that looked like a big silver platter stained dark at several places hanging outside the window. Suddenly the moon dissolved into a large, ugly mass of black and squeezed through the window. Reba was smothered under the heaps of black. She screamed. Little Rima woke up at the noise and began to cry. 'What happened? Why are you screaming? You have woken her up.' Rohit grumbled sleepily. Reba was startled out of her trance. She cast a cursory glance at the moon. It smiled happily in the distant sky, wearing a halo of silvery bright. The spots in it looked dull and faded. She lifted Rima into her lap and lulled her back to sleep.

Days became months and months slid into years. Rima was growing up, and the gap between Reba and Rohit was growing too. Everything looked normal and unchanged on the surface. But Reba knew that things were no longer the same as they used to be earlier. The night on which Rohit asked Reba to apply the skin care creams to get rid of the spots on her face had marked the beginning of that change.

Their worlds, Reba felt, had slowly drifted apart. Rima was the tie that kept the two connected to each other. Reba indulged herself in the upbringing of her daughter to get over the unconscionable belittlement. Rohit, despite being aware that Reba was trying to keep herself aloof, and that he was responsible for the change in her in one way or other, never made any effort from his side to bridge the emotional gap. They went out for dinner and movies occasionally but the flavour of that deep intimacy was missing.

The visions came time and again. The random, disjointed pictures of the water-mirror of the pool in autumn, the big round moon and the deepening ugly spot on it, her spotless face gone weird in the stirring water of the pool, and on the onrushing wall, growing bigger and bigger until it became a blinding white mess......overlapped one another. She felt little lightheaded and skittish after every such hallucination. She began to squirm more and more into herself.

Something very mysterious happened one night. She was sitting on the bed after putting little Rima to sleep. Rohit was in the drawing room watching the highlights of a cricket match. From nowhere, a young girl emerged from just behind her and made her way towards the door. 'Hey, wait there! Who are you, how did you come here?' Reba, shocked out of her wits, strode after the girl. The girl did not stop and went out to the front gate crossing the drawing room. Reba followed her, trying badly to catch a glimpse of her face. The girl reached the front gate and opened it. She turns back and looked straight at Reba. Reba gaped at the girl's face. She had three patches on her face, exactly on the same areas where Reba had them, two under the eyes and one on the forehead. It looked exactly like the face of a young Reba. Reba saw that there were tears in the girl's eyes, her lips quivered as if she wanted to say something. Then she turned, and quickening her pace went out into the thick darkness. 'Stop, hey you!' Reba called out and ran after her. Two strong hands gripped her shoulders. Reba stopped and looked at the owner of the hands. 'What is all this? Who do you think you are calling?' Rohit asked, looking troubled. Reba blinked. She was standing by the front gate of their house. The street outside was deserted. 'How did I come here?' She asked more to herself than her husband. 'I am supposed to be in my bed, beside Rima.' It was a puzzle that baffled her. She followed Rohit into the hose, went to her bedroom without saying a word and flopped on the bed, feeling unusually tired. Rohit stood by the bed for some time, looking at her in concern. 'Go to sleep, and do not trouble your mind with absurd thoughts.' He said and left, closing the door behind him.

The incident was repeated two nights after. The girl appeared from nowhere and ran out of the house to the front gate and then disappeared into the night after casting a brief glance at Reba. This time it was Rima who brought her back to herself. 'Mama', 'Mama'......Rima called out. She was frightened not to see her mother by her side. Her loud cries brought Reba back to reality. She put Rima back to bed and sat beside her, thinking.

'What is the matter with me? Is it mere hallucination or something else?' A dreadful thought struck her with the force of a lightning. 'Am I sleepwalking?" She tried to drive the thought away, but it kept coming back. She did not tell anything about that night's incident to Rohit, but she guessed that Rohit too was thinking that she had developed some serious mental disorder.

It happened again a month later. She had walked up to the main gate in her sleep and was about to go out when the blare of the horn of a motor vehicle startled her back to her senses. This time, Rohit was visibly worried. 'I think we should consult a doctor or something. A psychiatrist may be.' He said guardedly.

'I am not mad, and I do not need a psychiatrist's counselling,' Reba snapped.

'But this must be treated by an appropriate doctor. You might bring harm upon yourself if you are not properly treated. Everyone who seeks a psychiatrist's advice is not mad,' Rohit tried to explain. But Reba was not convinced and dismissed the subject, afraid that more discussions on the subject might convince her that she had actually developed some serious mental issue.

Fortunately, the incident was not repeated for a long time. Rohit was feeling relaxed. He knew that a change had come over Reba since the time he had asked her to use the cosmetics for her patches. He was unable to understand why Reba reacted in this way. What offence had he done by making an effort to better the looks of his wife? But he did not mention the cosmetics again in years. Reba had thereafter, stopped attending Rohit's official parties. Nor did Rohit ask her to. Though he refused to admit it, and felt a bit guilty about it, he too felt more comfortable alone.

The breach was there. But they pretended to ignore it and let life move on its chartered course.

Rima had, in the meantime, grown up into a young and beautiful girl of thirteen. She was in class seventh now. She was a good at sports, as well as her studies. She also sang and painted. The principal of her school, and her teachers praised Rima highly in the parents-teachers' meetings which made Rohit and Reba proud. Of late, Reba had noticed Rima looked a bit disturbed when she went to her school to attend the parents-teachers meeting. Rima tried her best to hide her discomfiture, but it did not escape her mother's eyes. But Reba did not mention it to her.

It was the day of the annual function in Rima's school. She was participating in a dance program and was quite excited about it. Reba, too, was excited to see her lovely daughter performing.

Rima walked into the room. Reba had spread out a number of saris on the bed, and was trying to select one to wear in the function. 'What are you doing, Mama?' she asked without much enthusiasm. Reba noticed that Rima was looking a little disturbed, but she did not mention it. 'Come, dear! Help me in selecting a good sari. I am so confused!

'Why do you want to select a sari? Where are you going?'

'What do you mean by that? Obviously to the annual function of your school!'

Rima was silent for a while. Then she spoke, a bit haltingly, as if it needed a lot of effort to say what she intended to say.

'I don't think you should go there, Mama,' she said at last.

'But why?' I always go to your annual functions. Don't I?

'This time no one's parents are coming.'

'And why is that?'

'I and my co-performers have decided that way,' Rima muttered trying to sound convincing. 'We feel that the presence of parents will distract us. We may feel conscious and make gross mistakes on account of that. You may come after my performance if you like.'

'What's the use? I wanted to see you performing. But then, you are right. The presence of parents might distract you from giving your best. Okay. I will not go. Put in all your efforts to make it the best performance,' Reba said and looked at her daughter. The look of relief on her face was like a knife stab. 'Please, do not mind, Mama! Rima smiled weakly and went out of the room.

Reba flopped on the bed. Her ears felt hot. Her throat was dry. She had guessed why Rima did not want her presence among the guests. She had grown old enough to feel embarrassed by the ugly looks of her mother. She had tried to prevent her from attending the function with a pretext that was childlike and implausible.

She lay face up on the bed and stared up at the whirring ceiling fan, seeing nothing.

Rima left after lunch for the stage rehearsal.

'Why aren't you ready till now? It is already five thirty. We will get late for the function,' Rohit said. He had returned from office early to attend the annual function. Rima had not told him what she told her mother about the quality of performance getting compromised because of the presence of the parents. Reba knew that Rima felt happy to introduce Rohit as her proud father.

'I have a bad headache,' Reba lied. 'I am afraid I can't make it,' she said lazily. 'You have to go alone. She might feel bad if neither of us go.'

'Okay. You take rest,' Rohit said.

'How comfortable they both feel when I am not around!!' A hard sob rose to her throat choking her.

She stood by the window and watched Rohit leaving. Then she walked back to the leaving room and sprawled on the comfortable lounging chair. She dozed off.

The harsh sound of the doorbell brought her awake. She slid off the lounging chair and went to the front door. She opened the door. Their cook, Sujata was standing outside. 'Were you asleep Madam? I have been ringing the bell for quite some time.' Reba stood aside to let her in.

She instructed the cook about the dinner and returned to the bed room.

She switched on the TV and sat back on the bed. She looked at the lighted screen but her mind registered nothing. After an hour and a half or so the cook completed her dinner and left. She locked the front door. It was going to be nine O' clock. Rohit and Rima would not be returning for at least an hour. Now her head actually began to ache.

She switched off the light and sat on the bed, resting her back against the pillow. Her headache was getting worse. She got up and took out a pain killer pill from the medicine box, turned off the TV and lay down. She thought about her daughter who, despite all her efforts to hide the truth that she felt embarrassed to be seen with her mother, had failed pathetically. Rohit, too, did not persuade her to accompany him to his official get together meetings or business parties for the same reason. She did not blame either Rima or Rohit for that. But she nourished a secret wish to feel the touch of the feather tip on her face and hear the loving voice telling her to look in the water mirror. She wanted to see the reflection of her face there, beautiful, spotless and glowing. She buried her face in the pillow and cried her heart out. She felt a little light and exhausted from the crying and drifted into sleep.

The doorbell rang. Reba turned on her side groggily and squinted at the wall clock. The hands showed forty minutes after nine. 'They have come back,' she said to herself. She was not expecting them before ten thirty. The bell rang again, this time a little impatiently. She got down and walked to the front door.

A girl stood outside the door. She looked familiar. Reba looked searchingly at her face. There were three distinct dark patches on her face, one under each eye and one on the forehead. Reba bent down a little to have a closer view of the girl. She looked like a small replica of Reba herself.

'Let's look at our faces in the pool? Our bright and unblemished faces... you know the pool never lies. Come with me.' The girl turned and walked towards the gate. Reba looked up. A half-moon shone brightly in a cloudless sky. She did not have the heart to say 'no' to the girl. She looked so innocent and vulnerable. 'Wait for me,' she called out after the girl and followed her.

They walked on. The road was deserted. The leaves of the trees that stood lined up on both sides of the road whispered mysteriously. 'How far it is?' Reba asked. Her legs were beginning to ache. 'We are almost there,' the girl replied without looking back.

Suddenly, out of nowhere a big grey wall appeared blocking the path. Reba could see the twin faces on the wall, one was the girl's and the other was her own. The faces had no patches on them. She stared at the faces and they were transformed into two blindingly bright circles. The girl walked straight into the wall and vanished. "Don't,' Reba screamed and rushed after her. The twin circles of light engulfed her. There was a white, hot explosion inside her brain and then darkness, thick and heavy, descended on her.

It was about four O' clock in the morning.

Rohit and Rima sat on the porch. Rima was whimpering into her palms. Rohit's eyes were burning dry. It was more than an hour since the ambulance had left carrying Reba's body. The crowd had dispersed.

The police men too had gone back. They had taken the young man who was driving the car and surrendered, into custody and had seized the car.

The friends and relatives would be arriving soon.

Rohit turned his gaze towards the house. Most of the lights were on. The house appeared very empty in that desolate luminescence. After Reba had taken back all the darkness into her own shadow circle, the big house that stood like a ghost on the ruins of memory, looked white and hollow.

*****

Face of the Morning

I am not superstitious the way most people are. But I must admit that I am a bit prejudiced about certain things. People nourish several sorts of blind beliefs. If a person sneezes or someone calls you back while you are going out it is believed that the purpose of your journey will not be fulfilled. A similar fate awaits your journey if a cat crosses your path.

I am not very serious about those things. But there is one thing I am particular about, seeing a good face in the morning.

The first look at a face in the morning, I tend to believe, determines the fate of your day. If it is a good face, the day passes smoothly, hassle free. A glimpse of a bad face in the morning spoils the entire day.

I cannot, of course give a convincing answer to the question that what made this prejudice grow so strong in me because I cannot date it back accurately.

Nor can I be very specific about the parameters for judging the auspicious or inauspicious quality of a face. Maybe it was the incident of my poor performance in English test in my school finals that generated such a belief. That morning as I was starting out after saying my prayers, from nowhere a man appeared at our front gate. He wore a shabby singlet type of affair over a pair of shabbier looking trousers. A dirty cloth-towel slung from his shoulder.

'Namaskar Sana babu,' 'he greeted me bowing a little, and entered the compound. I did not say a word and headed for my school riding my bicycle, troubled with premonitions. As such I have terrible misgivings about the English paper and this unexpected incident had filled me with foreboding. As was expected the paper was tough and I had to leave two questions unanswered. All my anger resulting from frustration vented against the rustic looking face I had seen in the morning while I opened the front gate.

'How did the paper go?' Father asked when I reached home.

'Average' I said haltingly. ' Tough questions.'

'You only know to blame the question setter. Ever given a thought to the lacking in your preparation? Well, try to do better in the rest of the papers.'

My father is a man of few words. He did not stretch the matter any further, but his dissatisfaction was quite evident in those few sentences he spoke. I felt even more frustrated. Later I learned that the man I met at the front gate in the morning was a croft farmer who did the farming in our land. He had come to give my father's share of money obtained from the selling of the annual yield. But I had developed a sort of abhorrence towards him. I strongly believed that he only was responsible for my poor performance in the paper that day. I avoided looking at his face all the time he was there at our home.

I had more than one bitter experiences with faces that bring bad luck. I can clearly recollect the day I had escaped an accident that could have been serious. From nowhere a beggar woman had come to beg in our street. Every day early morning she would go from house to house carrying a dented aluminium bowl and asking for money and rice. I disliked her at the first sight. She had a conical face, deeply lined and weather beaten. The mass of the frizzy, windblown hair that framed her face gave it a weird look which I repelled from. Added to that she had an irritatingly screechy voice.

Though she was a middle-aged woman she walked with the support of a bamboo stick, to fake, I believed, a physical disability and gather sympathy from people. My mother used to give her rice and vegetables and some money. That might be the reason the woman never missed her visit to our house every morning. The window in my room overlooked the compound and the front gate. The first thing I did every morning was to shut the window to prevent an accidental glance at the woman's face. I opened it only after I came back from college. But on that important day of my life, God knows how, I had forgotten to shut the window. That day I was to attend an interview for a job. I was both excited and nervous. Mother came in carrying my breakfast. She also brought curd and sugar in a small bowl. 'Curd and sugar bring good luck, ' she said. It was impossible to eat anything. Anxiety was giving me collywobbles. But mother would not give up. She made me eat a little something somehow. However, she was very particular that I finished the sugar added curd.

As I was about to slide my hand into the wrist watch band my gaze involuntarily turned towards the window. And there she was, looking straight at me!!

My heart skipped a bit. 'Oh, my God!! What a

blunder I have committed! How could I forget to shut the window on such an important day of my life?' I kept cursing myself. But the damage was done and there was no possible redressal at that point of time. I went to the puja room, begged the gods to protect me from the adverse impact of this unexpected encounter. My sister gave her some money and she went away. I waited for her to go out of the sight and then started off on my bike.

There was not much traffic on the road. I was driving at an average speed. But my mind was in a turmoil. The beggar woman's face had substantially added to my anxiety. Suddenly a small boy ran in front of my bike to the other side of the road. I was caught off guard and pressed the brake with all my strength. The bike, under the impact of the sudden brake, skidded to left side of road. I pitched forward and crash-landed on the sand verge. A small crowd gathered around me. Hands lifted me and I sat up with an effort. It was a miracle that my helmet was still on my head even after that nasty fall. Except for a few scratches on my hand and face I was alright. My legs were trembling badly, and it took me sometime to stand up steady. A couple of young men lifted my bike and started it. The bike was okay, too. It was a close shave. I thanked God for saving me and rode off to the venue of the interview. I was sure by this time that there was no point in attending the interview and trying to reach the place in time would be a wasted effort. The beggar woman's repulsive looking face had taken care of that. Needless to say, my performance in the interview was not up to mark. I knew I had lost the job.

My family was so worried about my accident that my interview was totally forgotten. 'Jobs would come and go,' my mother said. 'It is more important that God had saved you!' Tears of gratitude ran down her eyes as she ran her hand affectionately on my head. Father did not ask me a word about the interview. He was more anxious to take me to a doctor and get me properly examined. Despite my pleadings that I had no internal injury, and I was fine, he drove me to the swanky clinic of his friend who was a medicine specialist. He was a little satisfied after a CT scan, and a thorough investigation were done. The doctor congratulated me on my narrow escape and wished me luck.

The next morning, the beggar woman routinely walked up to the front gate, calling 'Ma,' in her gritty voice, as she did in all other days. My sister came out carrying a bowl of rice. Before she could reach the front gate, I ran out and stopped her. 'I will give it. You go inside.' My sister looked at me with astonished eyes as she handed the bowl to me. 'You? She asked in disbelief. But you have never ...' she did not complete the sentence and walked back into the house.

I walked to the front gate carrying the bowl of rice. She held out her dented aluminium pot and I poured the rice into it.

'Wait,' I said as she was about to move away. She stopped abruptly. 'Do not come here begging again,' I warned her through gritting teeth. ' I will teach you a lesson you will never forget if I saw you at our gate even for once!' I said menacingly. She did not say anything and looked straight at me. There was a queer look in her eyes. It was difficult to decipher the look. It could be anything...., resentment, disappointment, disdain.

But I did not bother. I had lost a good job on account of her. And I had escaped a serious accident by inches. I was not going to forgive her.

She did not come to our house the next day or the day after. Soon she stopped visiting other houses on the street. 'Good riddance,' I thought. But there was something that nagged at my conscience. Had I been too rude to her? I fought the thought back. 'That beggar woman has not been around for a long time. Where has she gone?' My mother wondered. 'She must have found out some other houses in some other area. These people have a nomadic nature,' my sister remarked.

'She was a nuisance. A look at her ugly face in the morning ruins the day. It is good that she has moved on to some other place,' I remarked.

'Why do you think like that? Poor thing! She was just asking for a little rice and some money. Hope she is fine wherever she is!' My sister sounded unhappy.

'It was because of her I met with an accident that day. I was not selected for the job because I saw her face while going out for the interview that morning. I tell you she is evil!' I snapped at her.

'You are only looking at the wrong side of things. Why can't you presume that it is because you had started off seeing her face you had had such a close shave? You are perhaps destined for a better job in future times. That might be the reason why you were not selected in the interview.' My sister tried to explain. But I could not agree with her. 'Well, I can't be a goody-goody like you,' I sneered. 'So, stop philosophizing!'

She made a face at me and left the place.

++++++

Eventually I got appointed in a multinational company at Bangalore. In the beginning it was not easy to leave the comforts of home and settle at a strange, big city. I felt homesick in my initial days in the new place. But slowly I got acclimatized with the working ambience and made a few good friends. It was not difficult to get an accommodation. I shared a three-bedroom kitchen and hall apartment with two of my colleagues in a reasonably well-put building that was not far from my office. Life was going easy except for the pressure of work, but I knew that had to be taken in stride. The apartment we lived in was on the sixth floor of a multi storied structure. Right in front of our flat lived a decent Gujrati family of a husband and wife and two school going daughters. The Patels were decent and courteous. The younger one, Loyla, was seven and studied in standard two in a renowned public school. Every morning around six O clock when I went out for the morning walk, she would be standing there by the entrance of the apartment building accompanied by either of her parents waiting for the school bus. I took an instant liking to the girl on the very first morning I saw her. 'Wish uncle good morning', her father said to her. The girl smiled and did as her father asked her to do. There was something in her little lovely face that made me believe that this was the face that would bring me luck.. Thereafter it became a routine to cast a glance, however brief it might be, at her face before starting my day. Though nothing exceptionally good occurred but nothing untoward also happened on those days. I felt uncomfortable on the weekend mornings because she would not be there to raise the level of my enthusiasm.

The apartment on the right to the elevator had remained unoccupied for a long time. The owner, I understood, had settled abroad. He had engaged a caretaker who came at intervals to clean the house and keep it in shape.

On one Friday evening as I was unlocking the door to our flat I noticed that the door of the apartment was open. I could hear voices in the house too. Perhaps the owner had come for a short visit, I guessed.

I asked Mr. Patel about the visitor of the apartment on the right side of the elevator the next morning when he stood waiting for the school bus with Loyla at the front entrance. 'The owner is one Mr. Subramaniam who has settled in UK for the last five years. His parents lived here in this flat. After his father's death Mr. Subramanian took his mother to UK. Now he has brought back his mother who insisted to spend the rest of her life in the house where she had lived with her husband. He would make the necessary arrangements for his old mother to live in comfort here and return in a week or so. He has engaged a cook, two nurses who would take care of the lady in the day and night shifts by turn, a maid to run errands and a housekeeper. A cousin of Mr. Subramanian who has a job here and lives with his family will supervise the things here.'

I was curious about the new arrival, the old woman who preferred living alone here than staying with her son. 'She must be one who values freedom over the ostentatious concern of a son and daughter in law.' I thought.

A few days passed. Occasionally while stepping into or out of the elevator I happened to catch a flitting glimpse of a middle aged woman and another young woman, who I guessed might be the cook and the nurse, through the semi open door of the front room. I came to know from Mr. Patel that the son, Mr. Subramanian had left for UK. I did not know why but I was a bit uneasy about the presence of an old woman, who I had learnt from Mr. Patel, was above eighty, on the same floor. He told me that the woman was fit and healthy despite her advanced age.

I saw her one morning as I was leaving for the office. I stood near the elevator space waiting for it to come up. The door of the apartment to the right opened and an old lady poked her face out through the half open door. I was not prepared for this sudden face to face meeting with her since it had become a routine for me to take a look at Loyla's face the first thing in the morning. The old lady smiled at me, a fond, amiable smile. I joined my palms and wished her politely.

'God bless you my son,' the old lady said. She had a sweet voice and a perfect, flawless pronunciation. She must be very good looking in her prime youth, I thought as I took in her aquiline nose, thick, arched eyebrows and big eyes at one short glance. The thick mass of her white hair was held in a neat bun at the back of her head. She exuded an aura of aristocracy. 'You are on this floor? ' She asked. 'Yes, 603, I replied.

'Your parents are here, too?'

'My parents are in, Odisha'.

I know Odisha, a beautiful province. Rich culture.' She remarked. 'You are doing a job here?' She continued, eager to carry on a conversation. But I was feeling discomfited in her presence. 'God knows what awaits me today now that I have seen this old woman's face while starting for office. 'Yes, in an IT company,' I said and strode into the elevator the moment its doors slid open, and pressed my finger on the 'G' button. I was feeling so disturbed that I could not greet Loyla in my usual cordial way and just managed to force a smile.

Nothing untoward or unusual happened in the office that day. I and my room mates had planned to cook egg curry for dinner. I was given the charge of getting eggs while returning home. I stopped the bike in front of the egg and chicken shop and bought the eggs. I paid the man and walked to the spot where I had parked my bike. I was about to open the dickie of the bike when the lights went out. The area was plunged into darkness. A scooter sped past me missing my foot by inches. In the confusion the paper carry-bag containing the eggs slipped from my hand. And the lights came back. I stared down at the bag of eggs that lay by the hind wheel. The egg fluid, a blend of white and yellow was oozing thickly out of it. There was no point in picking up the bag and examining the contents. I went back to the shop to buy eggs. Suddenly a strange thought like a flash of lightning crossed past my mind. 'Did it happen because I had seen the face of the old woman in the morning?' But I tried to reason out. I could not just link all the big and small troubles that come up in a day to a face I see in the morning. And who knows, like my sister used to debate, the trouble could have been serious had it not for the face that appeared before the eyes at the beginning of the day? What if the wheel of the scooter had run over my foot? No doubt some amount of money was waisted in re-buying the eggs but that was much better compared to the other possibilities. The agitation in my mind had considerably calmed down by the time I reached the entrance of our apartment building. I rode up to the sixth floor and was surprised to find the door of our flat open. Binay and Amrit were watching the highlights of an old cricket match in the front   room. 'What happened? Why are you sitting here? What about cooking? It is going to be nine O' clock. Come on, I am hungry. Let's start. I have got the eggs.' I said. 'We are hungry too, bro! ' Amrit laughed. But no cooking tonight. No gas. So, we will have to go out for dinner. We were waiting for you. Change quickly and come.'

No gas? I asked bitterly. 'You know I had to buy double the number of eggs because the first lot got damaged.' I narrated the episode of the sudden power failure and the breaking of the eggs,'

'Tch, tch ,' Binay chuckled. 'That is really bad. Now stop brooding over it and get ready. I am famished!' Nothing unusual had happened, I thought lying on my bed. Everything was a normal occurrence.... the eggs getting damaged and the cooking gas cylinder going empty. But I could not get the uneasy feelings out of my mind. Two negative things happening almost simultaneously could not be a coincidence. But we had enjoyed the dinner. It might be the reason why the gas was finished before time. It could always be given a positive twist. I felt relaxed after I put it in that perspective. But I religiously avoided facing Mr. Subramanian's mother since the next day.

++++++

A month passed without any significant happening. I met Loyala and Mr. Patel at the main entrance on all mornings barring the school holidays of course. The office environment was reasonably conducive.

There was one snag, however. I had been in the company for near about two years and my promotion to the next cadre was long overdue. A raise in the salary and additional perks would accompany the promotion. But God only knew why, the boss sat tight on the file blocking it. More than once I had reminded him politely about the badly delayed promotion. His answer to me would be some stupid non-convincing explanation which neither I nor he believed in.

It became more painful when my roommate Binay got promoted to the next cadre. Binay and I had passed out from the same B school in the same year scoring nearly similar percentage. Incidentally, we got jobs in the same city though in different companies. It was quite unjust that he was chosen for promotion and not I.

Every morning as I started off looking at Loyala's smiling face, a hope surged in me. I expected one of my colleagues would greet me cheerfully at the door and break the news of my promotion. But nothing like that happened in days. Even Loyala's bright smile did not help any.

+++++++

It was a rainy Monday. I was not in a mood to get up leaving the cosy warmth of the bed. Besides, I had, in the past few months, had lost the earlier enthusiasm of going to the office. But I knew there was no respite. I dragged myself out of the bed and went through the routine brush, bath, toilet and shaving. I made myself a cup of black coffee and went out. Both Binay and Amrit had already left. As I was locking the front door, the door of Mr. Subramaniam's flat opened. My gaze turned involuntarily towards it. Mr. Subramanian's mother stood at the door. She was looking directly at me. 'Nasty weather! Isn't it?' She flashed a smile at me. She looked beautiful and young when she smiled. 'Good Morning' I said. 'Nasty weather indeed!' I said because I had to say something in response. It would have been rude and unmannerly if I had left without making a response. I strode into the elevator without giving her a scope to lengthen the conversation. Besides I was late that morning and I did not want to offer an explanation to Mr. Wadekar, our boss, who was very particular about punctuality.

I reached the office about ten minutes late. As I was stepping into the elevator in a hurry, the lift man approached me with an apologetic smile. 'The elevator is not working, sir. The company mechanics would be arriving now. But you must use the stairs for the time being.'

'Here comes the first blow,' I thought bitterly, 'the consequence of meeting Madam Subramanian in the morning. God knows what else is there in store.'

I hurried up the stairs wishing to God that the boss would not take notice of my belated arrival. The first person I met at the office entrance was Juben. I wondered why he was not in his cubicle. It was going to be nine thirty. Everyone was supposed to be in their seats their eyes glued to the computer screen at this time.

'Guess what,' he said his eyes twinkling as if he was going to reveal a great secret. 'What?' I looked at him questioningly.

'Here is the breaking news, buddy!' Dhruv announced in mock solemnity. 'The boss is leaving for Sweden tonight. He will be there for at least six months. Mr. Vasudevan will take over in his absence.

It was good news indeed. The boss was a real bully. Everyone was exasperated with him. Everyone was working under stress and wanted him out of the scene. This piece of news came as a huge relief to all of us. Mr. Vasudevan was a nice gentleman with a pleasant personality. It was indeed a welcome change. All of us got busy in preparing for the send-off party in the evening and I had completely forgotten Madam Subramanian. I remembered her only after reaching the apartment. The lights in her apartment were out. She was an early sleeper as most of the people of her age.

A look at her face in the morning, I had always presumed, would ruin my day. It was a surprise that the day proved a good one for me. Even the elevator was mended by midday. I kept awake for a long time, my mind churning the incidents of the day. Perhaps Madam Subramanian did not cast a negative influence as I believed. I was still wondering if she was a bad omen or not when I drifted into sleep.

An uneventful month passed. Life at the workplace had turned out congenial in the absence of Mr. Wadekar. Mr. Vasudevan, by nature was accommodative and accessible without being lenient. I hoped he would not be unreasonably rigid about my promotion as Mr. Wadekar was. But despite his geniality the new boss did not seem to be any enthusiastic about the promotion or a raise in the salary of his employees.

I was getting more and more impatient. One morning I again met Madam Subramanian in the corridor. She was taking a walk in the corridor with the support of the young nurse. She looked pale and sick. I wondered what made her look so bony and haggard in such a short time. 'Good morning beta, ' she smiled at me. Despite the pallor that had settled on her face, the smile had not lost its charm. For the first time I felt the edge of my conscience scraping me. ' She is a nice lady. Perhaps I was not right in believing her responsible for the problems that came in my way. Perhaps I was becoming too judgmental.' But somewhere in the depth of my heart a selfish instinct prompted me to blame her face for the bad luck that befell me. I greeted her with a polite good morning wish and strode down the stairs without waiting for the elevator.

I reached early that day. I seated myself in front of the computer and switched on the system. Sambit brisked into the office.

'Hey, buddy, do you know the good news? I have got my promotion. Received the mail an hour back.' He was all smiles and his eyes sparkled in joy. 'Congratulations buddy ', I hugged him. I was really happy for him. He was senior to me, and his promotion was long overdue. 'What I heard is Mr. Vasudevan is clearing the files. Your file may get cleared up soon.' Sambit said encouragingly.

'I may not be that lucky,' I replied feeling a little disappointed within and returned to my seat. We celebrated Sambit's promotion that evening in a three-star hotel. It was past eleven by the time I returned home. I kept awake for a long time, brooding over my predicament, feeling desperate. 'If they don't promote me by the end of this year I will quit here and join another better   paying company,' I decided before I slept. A month and a half passed without being significant in any manner. Slowly but steadily a sense of depression was taking grip over me. I began to while away time in the company of friends in parks and clubs playing cards and chess to get over the gloom without much effect. I usually returned late to the apartment. Amrit and Binay understood my desperation and were quite conciliatory in their approach and behaviour. Nothing helped, neither the affection and concern of friends nor the morning smile of Loyla at the gate. I had practically lost all hope and was feeling doomed.

++++++++

I was a bit surprised to find the lights in Mr. Subramanian's apartment on. I took out my mobile phone and checked the time. It was past midnight. The lights usually went off around ten in the night. There were many pairs of shoes and sandals outside the door. The obvious conclusion I could draw that Mr. Subramanian was on a visit to India. That explained the lights and the shoes at the door. 'I would meet him tomorrow before leaving for office,' I decided and unlocked the door to our apartment.

Voices were heard in the corridor. I looked groggily at the mobile screen. The time was five thirty in the morning. Who could be talking there in the corridor at this hour? I closed my eyes and tried to go back to sleep. I heard our front door opening. Must be Amrit. He had a snoopy nature. He too might have heard the voices and had opened the door to see what the matter was. I heard the door shutting minutes later, and then Amrit's voice. 'I do not know exactly what is going on, but the door of Mr. Subramaniam's apartment is open. Perhaps Mr. Subramaniam has arrived just now,' he said to Binay who was awake by that time. I slid off bed and came out of my room.

What is all these noises? I asked, splashing water to my face and eyes. ' It is Mr. Subramaniam,' Amrit said. 'He has arrived just now. That is why...' I went to the front room and peeped out. I saw Mr. Patel come out of his house. I opened the door a bit wider and wished him good morning and received a smiling response. 'Has Mr. Subramaniam come here?' I asked him in a small voice. He walked me to the far end of the corridor out of earshot. 'Madam Subramaniam was very sick. Her son has arrived last night. I think the old woman has passed away. But till now they have kept it all very hush hush.' At this moment Mr Subramaniam came out of the door. He looked pale and his eyes were heavy and red. Mr. Patel moved towards him. He put his hand gently on Mr. Subramaniam's back. Tears rolled down Mr. Subramaniam's eyes. ' I tried my best but could not reach here in time. The nurse and my cousin both say that she was calling my name even in her semiconscious state. I am so unfortunate a son. I could not be with her in her last moments.' Mr. Subramaniam said amidst sobs. Mr. Patel tried to console him. Madam Subramaniam's mortal body was to be carried to the cremation ground soon. An air of gloom hung over the apartment building. I wanted to go out of the place as early as possible. Amrit and Binay too were getting ready. The noise in the corridor grew louder. There were more voices. I opened the door and came out. I had decided to take the stairs to avoid further interaction. I stepped out and stopped.

They were just bringing her out. She was made to sit in a wooden chair decorated with a lot of flowers. Clad in a cream-coloured silk sari, her body and face washed, she looked very much alive. There was an expression on her face that reflected a mysterious contentment. A few drops of involuntarily tears escaped my eyes. Though I avoided meeting her in the morning she had, without my knowledge, carved out a small space for her in my heart. I remembered how her face lit up with a benign smile whenever she saw me. I remembered the way she called me beta(son) with a genuine fondness. I stood there my gaze fixed on her face, realizing with a prick at my heart that she would never come out of that door and wish me an affectionate good morning. They carried her down the stairs amidst the chanting of some slokas or something like that. Mr. Patel put a consoling hand on my shoulder. We were the only two left in the corridor that appeared strangely desolate. 'She was a good lady,' he said. 'Yes, she was,' I said and entered the elevator. I knew I was late. But I, somehow did not worry much about Mr. Vasudevan's reaction. I was feeling a bit empty inside as if I had lost something valuable forever.

'Here comes the man!!' Sambit announced cheerfully. It was followed by chortles from others. I looked at them, surprised at this sort of a greeting. Making me even more surprised Mr. Vasudevan came out of his cabin. 'Congratulations' he said flashing a broad smile at me and held out his hand. I shook hands with him. ' We want a party tonight, buddy, the real one! Not a pizza party on a roadside restaurant. I was beginning to guess what had happened. I had been promoted!! It was an occasion to be happy since I had lost hope. I should have been excited. But I did not feel much excitement inside, as if this long-awaited incident had suddenly lost all its charm. The face of Madam Subramaniam that looked so alive even in death kept returning to my mind. But I could not tell my friends about it. I gave them a treat, but I kept the celebration lowkey on the pretext that I was not feeling well. But they extracted a promise from me that there would be a real big party a few days after.

I returned at about twelve thirty. The building was plunged in a gloomy silence. My gaze turned automatically towards the door of the Subramaniams' apartment as I came out of elevator. The door was closed but a dim light came out through a small chink. The well lit corridor looked mysteriously deserted. I did not know why but I did something I had never done or wanted to do. I stood for a while by the elevator as if expecting the familiar figure to come out any moment and smile a blessing. I dragged my feet on to the door of my apartment. Then I heard the voice, distinct and loud. 'It is past midnight. You must not remain outside till this late, beta.' I swung on my heels sharply, a chill crawling up my nerves. The corridor looked empty and abandoned as before. No one was there. I unlocked the door with trembling hands and went in closing the door behind me. I could feel sweat trickling down from behind my ears. My roommates had gone to bed long since. I took a wash and slumped on the bed. I should have been happy that after a long wait I finally got the long overdue promotion. But it has lost all its charm now. How I had avoided meeting that old lady who lived here alone, far away from her only son! How she must have longed to have a small chat with someone who in some way could fill the vast emptiness she carried within her! And I resented her, afraid that a look at her face would ruin my day. I felt ashamed of myself. I lay on the bed, thinking of my selfishness, despising my own behaviour. Sleep was far away from my eyes. I tossed and turned on the bed for a long time. It was probably three o clock in the morning when finally, I drifted into an uneasy sleep.

Then I saw the large floor- to -ceiling mirror. And the faces slowly materializing in it. They were all there, Madam Subramaniam, the man from our village who used to come to our house at intervals, and the puckered beggar woman!! Their faces were clear one moment, and blurred and overlapping in the next. The beggar woman held out her dented bowl towards me, the shabbily dressed farmer from the village smiled kindly at me. Then there was Madam Subramaniam. She looked at me fondly. They all mumbled something in a chorus. But it was very indistinct. Like the faces the voices were all mixed up. Perhaps they were all saying the same thing, chanting something like 'Come on, son!! Come on son!' in a chorus.

Gradually It grew louder and louder and became a crescendo. I pressed my hands over my ears. I sat up on my bed, bathed in sweat. I found Amrit and Binay sitting there too, all smiles.

'Congratulations! Congratulations!' They said loudly. In my half asleep and half wakeful state it had sounded like 'Come on son. Come on son!'

I mumbled a brief thanks and promised a party. They left.

That day, for the first time in months, I did not hope to meet Loyla at the entrance of the building, as the elevator made its way down.

End

Black Eagle Books

www.blackeaglebooks.org
info@blackeaglebooks.org

Black Eagle Books, an independent publisher, was founded
as a nonprofit organization in April, 2019. It is our mission
to connect and engage the Indian diaspora and the world at
large with the best of works of world literature published on
a collaborative platform, with special emphasis on
foregrounding Contemporary Classics and New Writing.